"I'm worried about y

Her name on his lips sent a thrill of excitement rolling through Thea. A shiver of something she didn't want to name eased up her backbone and made her stomach flutter in awareness. She hadn't been attracted to a man in years. And now, at the worst possible time, with the worst possible man, Thea was feeling things she had no business feeling.

"Why can't you just go away and leave us alone?" she whispered.

His gaze softened, touched her lips, and Thea trembled, clutching her daughter's hand as if Nikki were her lifeline.

"There're some things about this case you may not be aware of. Have dinner with me and we'll talk about them."

Thea's heart started to pound. That she was even momentarily tempted by his invitation proved how dangerous he was to her.

She glanced down at Nikki. Nikki looked back up at her, her expression hopeful. The fact that Nikki showed a reaction at all was a positive sign. A small miracle.

With Nikki on his side, how on earth could Thea continue to do what she knew she must—resist John Gallagher?

Dear Intrigue Reader,

A brand-new year, the launch of a new millennium, a new cover look—and another exciting lineup of pulse-pounding romance and exhilarating suspense from Harlequin Intrigue!

This month, Amanda Stevens gives new meaning to the phrase "men in uniform" with her new trilogy, GALLAGHER JUSTICE, about a family of Chicago cops. They're tough, tender and totally to die for. Detective John Gallagher draws first blood in *The Littlest Witness* (#549).

If you've never been *Captured by a Sheikh* (#550), you don't know what you're missing! Veteran romance novelist Jacqueline Diamond takes you on a magic carpet ride you'll never forget, when a sheikh comes to claim his son, a baby he's never even seen.

Wouldn't you just love to wake up and have the sexiest man you've ever seen take you and your unborn child into his protection? Well, Harlequin Intrigue author Dani Sinclair does just that when she revisits FOOLS POINT. *My Baby, My Love* (#551) is the second story set in the Maryland town Dani created in her Harlequin Intrigue book *For His Daughter* (#539).

Susan Kearney rounds out the month with a trip to the wildest American frontier—Alaska. *A Night Without End* (#552) is another installment in the Harlequin Intrigue bestselling amnesia promotion A MEMORY AWAY.... This time a woman wakes to find herself in a remote land in the arms of a sexy stranger who claims to be her husband.

And this is just the beginning! We at Harlequin Intrigue are committed to keeping you on the edge of your seat. Thank you for your enthusiastic support.

Sincerely,

Denise O'Sullivan
Associate Senior Editor, Harlequin Intrigue

The Littlest Witness

Amanda Stevens

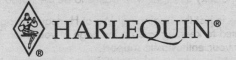

HARLEQUIN®

TORONTO • NEW YORK • LONDON
AMSTERDAM • PARIS • SYDNEY • HAMBURG
STOCKHOLM • ATHENS • TOKYO • MILAN • MADRID
PRAGUE • WARSAW • BUDAPEST • AUCKLAND

ISBN 0-373-22549-0

THE LITTLEST WITNESS

Copyright © 2000 by Marilyn Medlock Amann

This edition published by arrangement with Harlequin Books S.A.

® and TM are trademarks of the publisher. Trademarks indicated with ® are registered in the United States Patent and Trademark Office, the Canadian Trade Marks Office and in other countries.

Visit us at www.romance.net

Printed in U.S.A.

ABOUT THE AUTHOR

Amanda Stevens has written over twenty novels of romantic suspense. Her books have appeared on several bestseller lists, and she has won Reviewer's Choice and Career Achievement in Romantic/ Mystery awards from *Romantic Times Magazine*. She resides in Cypress, Texas, with her husband, her son and daughter, and their two cats.

Books by Amanda Stevens

HARLEQUIN BOOKS

2-in-1 Harlequin 50th Anniversary Collection
HER SECRET PAST

Don't miss any of our special offers. Write to us at the following address for information on our newest releases.

Harlequin Reader Service
U.S.: 3010 Walden Ave., P.O. Box 1325, Buffalo, NY 14269
Canadian: P.O. Box 609, Fort Erie, Ont. L2A 5X3

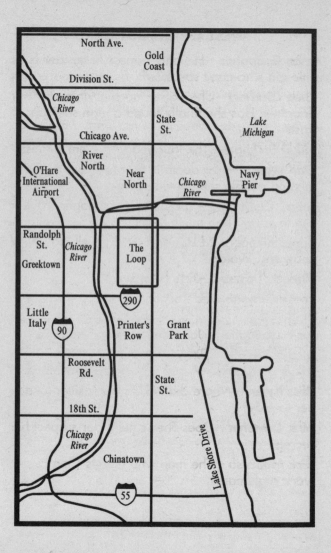

CAST OF CHARACTERS

John Gallagher — His only witness to murder is a little girl who can't speak.

Thea Lockhart — She's given up everything for her daughter. Has she finally found a man she can trust?

Nikki Lockhart — The four-year-old silent witness.

Gail Waters — Her death is as mysterious as the missing people she hunted down.

Morris Dalrimple — The building manager would like to know Thea *much* better.

Superintendent Ed Dawson — How well did he know Ms. Waters?

Annette Dawson — Ed's bitter wife.

Eddie Dawson — Ed's estranged son is nowhere to be found.

Liam Gallagher — John's uncle is in a hurry to close the case. Why?

Miles Gallagher — A cop with a faulty memory.

Bliss Kyler — Where did Nikki's baby-sitter take her to play?

Mrs. Lewellyn — Does Thea's neighbor suspect her secrets?

Rick Mancuso — The man who haunts Thea's worst nightmares.

This book is dedicated with much gratitude and
appreciation to my editor, Natashya Wilson.

Chapter One

Thea Lockhart hated being out so late. Every big city had its dangers, but Chicago after dark seemed particularly perilous, perhaps because she didn't yet feel at home there. Or perhaps because the weather was so cruel, even for November. The days were gray and dismal, spilling over into frigid nights that seemed to go on forever. Thea sometimes wondered if she would ever be warm again.

But the bone-deep chill came from neither the city nor the temperature. She could have gone anywhere— a southern city, a small town, even out of the country— and the demons would have followed, pursuing her to the ends of the earth if necessary.

Thea's fate—and her daughter's—had been sealed four months ago, when she'd fled Baltimore in the middle of the night, leaving behind her identity, her friends and family, and her ex-husband, dead on her bedroom floor.

Because of what she'd done, she and Nikki would be on the run for the rest of their lives. The Mancuso family, along with the rest of the Baltimore Police Department, would never stop looking for them. Thea had violated the Brotherhood, the Blue Wall, and for that she would pay dearly—if she was caught.

Shivering in her long wool coat, she hurried down Woodlawn Avenue, away from the university. The lake was only a few blocks away, and the icy wind whistled through the alleys, in sync for an eerie moment with an ambulance siren that built to a crescendo, then faded.

It was after midnight and the empty streets spooked her. A shiver of warning feathered up her backbone, but when she glanced over her shoulder, there was no one behind her.

Through a break in the buildings, she glimpsed the smokestacks from the power plant. They rose like dark guardians in the night sky, but if anything, the sight deepened Thea's chill. She felt alone and vulnerable. Exposed.

Normally she would have been home long before now, but three of the five waitresses scheduled for the evening shift at the diner had come down with the flu, and Thea's boss had pressed her into working a double.

As much as she hated not being home in time to bathe her daughter and put her to bed—an evening ritual that had become important to both of them—Thea couldn't refuse. Zelda Vanripper, owner of Zelda's Eatery in Hyde Park, had been good to her, putting her on the day shift so that she could be home with Nikki at night and asking few questions about her background.

So Thea had stayed and worked, and the extra tips would come in handy, as always. But after being on her feet since seven that morning, she couldn't wait to get home to a hot bath.

Her apartment building was only a few blocks from the diner, but the last two blocks dragged on her frazzled nerves and weary muscles. Huddling in her coat as a frigid gust tore at her, she hurried her steps, more anxious than ever to be out of the cold and the darkness.

As she crossed East Fifty-fifth Street, her apartment building finally came into view, but the sigh of relief died on her lips. Blue lights from half-a-dozen police cars bounced off the sides of buildings and reflected in long wavering beams down the wet street, capturing Thea in a frail azure glow.

She stood frozen for the longest moment, a two-word prayer rambling over and over in her mind. *Oh God oh God oh God.*

They'd found her!

Her first instinct was to turn and flee, to disappear into the shadows before anyone noticed her. But her daughter was in that building, and nothing, not even her own freedom, could compel her to run. She would never let them take Nikki back to Baltimore, back to the Mancusos, who would raise her in the same corruption in which they'd raised their own son.

Don't think about that now, Thea ordered herself, burying her trembling hands in her pockets. *Don't think about Rick or the gunshot or all that blood.*

Now was definitely not the time to panic.

Head down, shoulders hunched against the wind, she hurried along the sidewalk. When she drew near her building, she could see the area was cordoned off with yellow tape. Several policemen, uniforms and plainclothes, clustered around something in the street, almost directly in front of the building's entrance.

Thea's heart rocketed against her ribcage. Bile rose in her throat as she strained to see through the wall of policemen. *Please, God,* she prayed desperately. *Let Nikki be all right.*

If anything ever happened to her daughter, Thea wasn't sure how she would cope. Nikki was her whole life, a sweet damaged angel who had been put through hell because of her parents. Thea would do anything, *anything* to protect her.

But what if she was too late? What if Rick's family had somehow found them, and Nikki had tried to get away and…

Almost running now, Thea saw one of the officers step out of the way, and for the first time, she glimpsed the body lying on the pavement. Relief rushed through her when she saw it was a woman and not a child who lay motionless at the officers' feet. But in the next instant Thea realized with guilty compassion that the victim was someone's daughter. Her next of kin would be getting that terrible phone call, probably within the hour.

Lenore Mancuso's grief-stricken face flashed across Thea's mind, but she quickly shoved it aside. She wouldn't think about Rick's mother now, either.

Slowing, Thea hung back from the policemen, hoping they hadn't seen her. The cold air frosted their breath as they talked and laughed and went about their grisly business with the same disconnection Thea had always found so chilling in Rick.

Teeth chattering from the cold and from nerves, she walked past them, her head still bowed. But as she approached the stoop, one of the officers called out, "Hey, you!"

She hesitated and looked over her shoulder.

"Yeah, you. Come over here."

Her heart still pounding, Thea turned and slowly descended the steps. The officer met her at the bottom. He was one of the uniforms, middle-aged and heavyset, his face puffy and lined beneath the bill of his rain cap. His poncho billowed in the wind as he lifted his flashlight in her direction.

Automatically Thea turned her face away, but before he could switch on the beam, another car drove up and someone shouted, "Gallagher's here."

The man beside her muttered, "About damn time."

Thea hoped the newcomer would distract the officer so that she could slip away, but he turned to stare down at her in the rain. "You live in this building?"

Thea hesitated, then nodded.

"Out kind of late, aren't you?"

"I was just coming home from work." She bit her lip, trying to control the chattering of her teeth. "Wh-what happened?"

"Someone took a dive off the roof," the officer told her dispassionately. Then, "What's your name?"

"Thea Lockhart."

He carefully noted the information in his book. "Where do you work?"

"Zelda's Eatery. It's on East Fifty-seventh, near the university."

Thea expected more questions, but the officer seemed to lose interest as the lights on the unmarked car that had just driven up were killed. They both watched as a man—Gallagher, she presumed—got out. He was tall and his shoulders beneath the heavy overcoat looked enormous. In spite of the cold and the rain, he wasn't wearing a hat or gloves, and his coat flapped open in the wind, making him seem impervious to the brutal weather.

With grim deliberation, he surveyed the scene, his

gaze raking the whole area—including Thea—before he walked toward the body. There was no mistaking who was in charge now. The crowd of officers parted for him, and Thea got a clearer view of the victim. She hadn't expected so much blood. It reminded her of that night—

She staggered back a step and the policeman beside her caught her arm. "Hey, you okay?"

"I'm fine…"

But she wasn't. Violence and death hit too close to home, and as ashamed as she was to admit it, her main concern was how to disentangle herself from the police. She couldn't get involved. She felt sorry for the poor woman lying on the street, but she couldn't afford to get caught up in a police investigation.

Trembling, she watched as Gallagher knelt and examined the body. He didn't touch the victim, didn't disturb the crime scene with so much as a stray glance, but for a long moment, he remained there, studying her face as if her last thoughts might be lingering somewhere on her frozen expression.

After several minutes he stood. "Who was the first officer?" His tone was deep, authoritative. Not cold exactly, but a voice belonging to a man Thea had no wish to confront.

"McGowan," someone told him.

"Over here," the man beside her called out.

Gallagher turned and started toward them. His features stood out starkly in the streetlight. Even the rain didn't diminish the angles of his face, the broad nose, the full sensuous lips. His eyes were blue, which surprised Thea. She'd thought they would be dark, like his hair. The light color was particularly striking against his grave features.

He wore a suit beneath the overcoat, as if he'd taken the time to dress properly before coming out. But his cheeks were roughened with stubble, giving him a sinister appearance that made Thea's stomach quiver in fear.

His gaze barely grazed her before he said to McGowan, "What happened?"

"Wait here," McGowan told Thea. He and Gallagher took a few steps away from her, but the wind caught their voices and tossed them back at her. "Looks like a dry dive," McGowan told him. "DCDS. Detective Cox found a suicide note in her coat pocket."

"Any idea who she is?"

"Not yet. There's no ID on her, but Cox has gone up to canvass the roof for a purse or wallet, anything she might have dropped before jumping."

Almost inadvertently Thea's gaze followed Gallagher's to the roof of the building. She thought she could see someone up there now, and she shuddered as the shadow moved away from the edge.

"Who found the body?" Gallagher asked.

"The building manager. Claims he came outside just before midnight to walk his dog, and that's when he saw the victim lying on the street. He checked for a pulse, didn't find one and then went back inside to call 911."

"Great," Gallagher muttered. "Probably trampled all over anything resembling evidence." He paused. "Just before midnight you say. How accurate do you figure he is on the time?"

"Fairly accurate," McGowan told him. "He says he'd just finished watching an old episode of 'Hill Street Blues,' which comes on at eleven, but the closing credits hadn't yet run. He lives with his elderly mother. He says she can corroborate his story.''

"How soon did you respond?"

"Torecelli and I were on the scene within ten minutes after we got the call from dispatch. We secured the area and radioed for backup.''

"The manager couldn't identify her?"

McGowan shook his head. "Claims he never saw her before tonight. She's not a tenant, and he doesn't know how she got into the building, unless someone buzzed her in. The outside doors are always kept locked.''

That was true, Thea thought. But a policeman worth his salt knew how easy it was to obtain entrance to almost any unmonitored building. If someone wanted in badly enough, all he or she had to do was wait around until someone was either coming or going and slip through the unlocked door, usually unnoticed. Crooks did it all the time.

And so did murderers.

Thea shivered as she studied Detective Gallagher's grim countenance. His gaze traced the angle of the building, studying the windows that faced the street. "What about eyewitnesses?"

"None so far. No defense wounds, either, that we could see. We bagged her hands in plastic because of the rain.'' Thea knew that normally the police liked to use paper bags, because the lack of air with plastic could alter the evidence. But that was something she didn't want them knowing she knew.

In fact, the less any of them knew about her the better, especially Gallagher. Thea had a bad feeling about him. A very bad feeling.

He turned and observed the street again, watching

for a few minutes as the crime-scene unit finished taking pictures and then began scouring the ground around the body for trace evidence.

He glanced at Thea, then at McGowan. "Who's she?"

"She lives in the building. Says she was just getting home from work."

Gallagher nodded vaguely. "Might as well chalk the site when CSU finishes, although it won't do much good if the rain doesn't let up. I'm going up to the roof. Let me know when the coroner gets here. Establishing time of death is going to be a bitch in this weather."

McGowan nodded and took off, leaving Thea standing alone to face Gallagher. She hoped he'd just go up to the roof and forget all about her, but when he turned and started toward her, she saw in his eyes that he had no intention of letting her get away so easily.

"I'm Detective Gallagher." His gaze was direct, penetrating. If he noticed her trembling, Thea hoped he'd blame the cold. "And you are?"

"Thea Lockhart."

"Officer McGowan said you live in the building, is that right?"

She nodded. "I was just coming home from work when he stopped me."

"You work around here, Miss Lockhart?"

"It's…Mrs. I'm a waitress at a diner near the university. I already gave this information to Officer McGowan."

The detective's piercing gaze met hers. "You weren't home tonight?"

Thea shook her head, shoving her hands even deeper

into her pockets. "I've been away since before seven o'clock this morning. I didn't see anything."

"No strangers lurking around the building lately? No loud arguments, anything like that?"

"No, nothing unusual."

Gallagher nodded almost absently. "I wonder if you'd mind taking a look at the body. See if you can identify the victim."

The request was courteous enough, allowing her to decline if she wanted to, but Thea knew she had no real choice. No matter how much she didn't want to look at that poor dead woman, she mustn't do or say anything that might make Detective Gallagher suspicious.

She nodded and followed him over to the victim. The woman was lying on her back, her face surprisingly unscathed from what must have been a horrendous fall. But as Thea looked more closely, she saw the cuts and the terrible bruising that gave the body an almost ghoulish appearance. Her arms and legs were at strange angles, too, the bones undoubtedly shattered.

"I've never seen her before." But Thea had second thoughts almost at once. There *was* something vaguely familiar about the woman, but she couldn't place her. Which was good. At least she didn't have to tell an outright lie.

As if sensing her hesitation, Gallagher pressed, "You're sure?"

She could feel his gaze on her and she tried to suppress a shudder. "I don't remember seeing her around here before." Thea paused, then couldn't resist asking, "Do you really think she committed suicide?" Jumping from a building seemed like such a ghastly way to die, but then, so was a bullet to the heart. A sick feeling rose in Thea's throat, but she swallowed it away as she glanced up at Detective Gallagher.

His gaze narrowed on her, and she thought for one heart-stopping moment he might have recognized her. Then he said, "Suicide's a possibility. We'll know more when we've done a thorough search of the area. Right now you'd better get in out of this rain. We'll be in touch if we need you."

Alarmed, Thea started to ask why he would need to contact her again, but then realized he and the other officers would begin almost immediately the grueling work of talking to everyone in the building, searching for potential witnesses. *Goyakod,* Rick had always called it. Get off your ass and knock on doors. He would have been a good cop if he hadn't been dirty.

But Thea wouldn't think about that now. She'd become an expert at compartmentalizing her emotions, and right now all she would allow herself to concentrate on was getting away from Detective Gallagher without arousing his suspicions. She was desperate to go inside and check on Nikki.

She took the card he handed her, trying to control the trembling in her hands. But he noticed and said softly, "It's rough when you're not used to it."

If you only knew, Thea thought, but aloud she said, "I'm okay. I just need to be inside, out of the cold."

He nodded. "If you think of anything that might help, call me at that number."

Thea stuffed his card deep into the pocket of her coat, knowing all the while that Detective Gallagher would never get a call from her, no matter what. He was a cop, and that was all she needed to know about him. His badge made him one of the enemy.

SHE SEEMED AWFULLY NERVOUS for a bystander, John thought as he watched her at the front door of the building.

She dropped her keys on the stoop, and even from his position several yards away, he could see how badly her hands shook as she bent and picked them up. She started to insert her key into the lock, but then, realizing the door was already unlocked, she hurried inside. A pale blue scarf hid her hair while the oversize coat she wore wrapped her from neck to toe.

But even bundled up like that, John could tell she was a small woman. Petite, he supposed, would be the word. Her thin face was pale and translucent, her features—dark brown eyes, slightly crooked nose, full lips—almost fragile-looking.

There was something about her, apart from her obvious attractiveness, that intrigued him. She had the demeanor of a woman who had been badly frightened and was trying her damnedest to hide it. But if she didn't recognize the victim, what did she have to be scared of?

His inherent distrust was working overtime tonight, he decided, scowling. A lot of people were nervous around the police. Maybe the real reason Thea Lockhart triggered his distrust was that she reminded him a little of his ex-wife.

Meredith hadn't cared for cops, either. At least that was what she'd said the night she walked out. But then two months later, she'd married another one, leaving John to conclude that it was one cop in particular she hadn't cared for. Even though they'd been divorced for nearly two years, her betrayal still rankled.

But Meredith Clark was no longer his concern, and Thea Lockhart was probably just the nervous type, someone who fell apart at the sight of blood. The only woman John had to worry about now was the Jane Doe lying mangled on the concrete.

"Where's the building manager?" he asked the officer nearest him. "We'll need to start knocking on doors ASAP."

"He's on the roof with Detective Cox," the uniform told him. "Want me to radio up?"

"I'm headed that way." John took another look at the victim. Had she jumped off the building of her own free will or had she been pushed? In spite of the note found in her pocket, John voted for the latter. His every instinct told him this was a homicide, and if his hunch panned out, the next forty-eight hours would be critical. After that, the trail would start getting cold. If a case wasn't solved in the first two days, odds were good it would never be cleared. John knew that better than anyone.

"Hell of a night for a murder," he muttered as the rain started coming down harder.

Chapter Two

The rain peppered John's face as he stood on the roof, his presence as yet unnoticed. The wind was stronger up here, and he braced himself as he watched Cox's flashlight beam moving about the area.

The roof was surrounded by a concrete safety ledge, about three feet high and six inches wide. Near the stairwell door and to the left, pallets of building materials and twenty-gallon drums had been stacked in preparation for resurfacing and waterproofing the deck, but the rest of the roof was clear and open. But even so, at this time of night and in this weather, the prospect of an eyewitness was pretty dim.

John's gaze tracked his partner's progression across the roof. Roy Cox was a fifteen-year veteran of the Detective Division. He and John had been working together for nearly four years now, and although they couldn't have been less alike in temperament and investigative techniques, the partnership had worked out well. Whereas John was intense, almost obsessive about their cases, Roy was laid-back and soft-spoken, his west-Texas drawl as pronounced as it had been the day he'd left El Paso nearly thirty years ago.

He was a tall man, wiry and grizzled, with a handlebar mustache that might have looked more at home on a Texas range than it did on the streets of Chicago. A second man, the building manager, John guessed, dogged Cox's steps, his gravelly voice muted by the rain and wind. John switched on his flashlight, catching the man in his beam. Wide-eyed and startled, he looked like a deer trapped in headlights.

Cox called out, "Hey, that you, Johnny boy? Glad you could finally make it. I reckon even you gung ho-types have trouble tearing yourselves away from a warm body on a night like this."

John refrained from telling him that the only female in his bed lately was Cassandra, the temperamental Persian Meredith had left behind when she'd moved out. But Cox was his partner, and a nosy one at that; John suspected he already knew. "McGowan said you found a suicide note on the victim."

"Damn straight we did." Cox walked over and handed the bagged note to John. The words had been typed on a sheet of plain white bond paper.

"Short and sweet," John muttered, training his light on the note.

"Just the way I like my women." Cox grinned, his face pale in the cast-off glow from his flashlight. Water dripped from the brim of Cox's cowboy hat, the battered one he always wore in inclement weather. "Looks like this is our lucky night, Johnny."

"What do you mean?"

Cox held up a second plastic bag and aimed his flashlight beam on the contents—an expensive-looking beige handbag. "Found it on the deck over there by the wall. Victim must have dropped it just before she jumped. We've ID'd her from her driver's license."

"Who is she?"

"Name's Gail Waters. She had a press pass..."

The name hit John like a physical blow. Stunned, he stared at his partner as a shock wave rolled through him. "Who did you say?"

Cox gave him a quizzical glance. "Gail Waters."

Son of a bitch, John thought, trying to hide his surprise.

Cox rubbed the salt-and-pepper whiskers on his chin. "I'm getting some bad vibes here, Johnny-O. Are you trying to tell me you *knew* the victim?"

"I never saw her before in my life," John answered truthfully. But he knew the sound of her voice. He'd talked to her on the phone less than forty-eight hours earlier, when she'd called the station wanting to interview him about his father's disappearance seven years ago. It was a case that had not been solved to this day.

Gail Waters had been a reporter for and the managing editor of a small newspaper on the near north side of town. She specialized in stories involving disappearances and missing persons. Although she was a print journalist—and had taken pride in pointing out that fact to John—she had also been the co-producer of a cable show called *Vanished!*, which explored intriguing cases the police hadn't been able to solve.

Why she'd suddenly decided to investigate Sean Gallagher's disappearance, John had no idea. But her death had to be a coincidence. It couldn't have anything to do with his father.

But even so, names from John's past flashed like a strobe through his head: Ashley Dallas, the young woman whose murder Sean had been investigating at the time of his disappearance; Daniel O'Roarke, the man convicted of Ashley's brutal murder, who now sat on death row; and John's own brother Tony, who had been in love with Ashley at the time of her murder.

For some reason Gail Waters had wanted to dig up that old tragedy, expose secrets that had been buried for more than seven years.

And now she was dead.

A coincidence, John told himself again. But a cold finger of dread traced up his backbone as he stood in the icy rain.

"You want to notify the old man or should I?" Cox was asking.

The "old man" Cox was referring to was John's uncle and their commanding officer. Liam Gallagher kept himself apprised of every investigation the detectives conducted under his watch. His knowledge of all the uncleared cases in his jurisdiction was nothing short of phenomenal, and John had always held his uncle in the highest esteem.

But now a tiny doubt began to niggle at him. Liam had worked on the Ashley Dallas case, too. Had Gail Waters talked to him about John's father's strange disappearance?

"Let's hold off on that." John stared at the note for a moment longer, then handed it back to Cox. "A typewritten suicide note always worries me. I'd like to do a little more digging before we call in."

Cox groaned. "I don't like the sound of that. You're going to get a hard-on about this one, aren't you? You've got that look."

"I'm going to do my job," John said grimly. "And so are you. Until we get the coroner's report, we're going to treat this as a homicide investigation."

Cox muttered an oath as his radio crackled. He pulled it from his belt and walked a few feet away to respond. John used the opportunity to examine the wall and floor of the roof at the spot from where he judged the victim had fallen. Slipping on a pair of latex gloves, he knelt and scoured the area with his flashlight, knowing all the while the rain had probably washed away whatever trace evidence, including fingerprints, that might have been left.

"Meat wagon's here," Cox called from the stairwell door. "You coming?"

"I'll be there in a minute." John stood and gazed over the side of the building. Down on the street, a handful of bystanders had gathered at the fringes of the yellow tape.

As if sensing John's gaze, one of them, a man wearing a black parka, a stocking cap and a muffler covering the lower part of his face, glanced up at the roof. Even five stories away, John felt a tug of recognition.

He knew the man only as Fischer, an informant he'd used successfully in the past. John had no idea about the man's real identity, but he seemed to have an uncanny knack for showing up at crime scenes, particularly the ones John was called out on. He suspected Fischer not only had a police scanner, but an inside line into the department. Whatever his connection, his information had proved invaluable in the past.

As John watched, Fischer turned and headed down the street, his shoulders hunched against the sharp blast of wind from the lake.

John rubbed the back of his neck where the hair had suddenly stood on end. Fischer always gave him a case of the jitters, although he couldn't say why exactly. Maybe because there were elements of danger and distrust involved with all informants.

The door to the stairwell slammed shut in the wind

and Cox disappeared. John saw that the building manager remained and had started across the roof toward him.

He was a short squat man, somewhere in his forties, who breathed in sharp, almost gasping puffs of air. In the dim light he looked eager and excited, his small dark eyes greedily taking in every last detail of the search.

"Detective, if I may be so bold..." Rain glistened in the fringe of brown hair that circled the man's bald pate like a dingy halo.

"What is it?" John asked, annoyed at having his concentration broken.

"It's something I, er, mentioned to Detective Cox, but he, er, didn't seem to take much notice." The man stuttered and stumbled over his words, as if extremely nervous. He wiped moisture from his forehead with the back of his hand. "It's over there." He pointed to the stack of building materials near the stairwell door.

"What is?"

"I'm, er, not sure. Evidence maybe."

John said sharply, "What are you talking about, Mr.—"

"Dalrimple. Morris Dalrimple. My friends call me Dal."

"Why don't you show me what you're talking about, Mr. Dalrimple?"

The building manager touched his fingertips to his chin, then dropped his hand to his side. "I think I saw something. If you would, er, just shine your flashlight over there...a little more to your right...yes, that's it. Right there. And then if you would, er, kneel, like you did earlier..."

John complied, although there was something about

Dalrimple that was a little unsettling. To be honest, the man gave him the creeps.

John focused his light on the stacks of building materials. From where he knelt he could make out narrow channels running through the crowded pallets of drums. He didn't see anything at first, but then he moved the beam back, playing it along one of the channels.

"Yes, there it is!" Dalrimple cried excitedly. He almost jumped up and down with glee. "I thought I saw something in there earlier, although Detective Cox couldn't spot it. But if I may be so bold...tall people, er, tend to overlook a lot of things. You don't concern yourself with places that accommodate only little people—like myself, for instance. I thought right off the space between the pallets might be a good place for someone to, er, hide, but Detective Cox was certain no one could fit in there. I must admit, since I, er, put on a little weight, it might be a bit of a squeeze—"

Dalrimple broke off in midsentence as John stood and strode to the pallets. He bent and angled his light into the long channel between the stacks of drums. Something was lying on the floor several feet inside. Lifeless eyes gleamed in the crisp beam from John's flashlight.

John knelt and felt inside the channel. Using the flashlight as an extension, he dragged whatever was on the floor toward him, until he could reach it with his hand. His fingers closed around a scrap of fabric, and a tinny voice intoned, "Ma-ma" as he pulled a doll from its hiding place.

"Well, I'll be!" Dalrimple exclaimed, gazing down at the toy in John's hand. "How do you suppose that got in there?" He started to touch the doll's mop of dark hair, but John jerked it away. Dalrimple looked crushed.

"There could be prints," John felt obliged to explain. "You understand."

"Oh, of course. I know all about, er, police procedure. Mama and I never miss an episode of 'Cops.' So what do you think about the doll, Detective? Is it evidence?"

"Possibly." Walking back across the roof, he stood at the edge where Gail Waters had gone over and fixed his light on the stack of pallets. The channel between was tight, but as Dalrimple had suggested, a small adult could manage to squeeze inside. A child could do so quite easily. And if she had been hiding in the space earlier, she could have seen what happened without being detected.

It was possible he might have himself a witness, after all. And if Gail had been murdered, it was imperative that he find the owner of the doll as quickly as possible.

He turned to Dalrimple. "I'm going to need your help…Dal. This is very important."

The little man almost glowed. "Well, er, of course. Whatever I can do to be of, er, assistance."

"I'll need a list of all the tenants in the building, and I'll need you to flag the ones who have children. We'll start with the families who have little girls under the age of, say, ten."

Dalrimple's brow furrowed. "That could, er, take a while. I'm not so good on the computer, and Mama doesn't like to be disturbed once she's gone to bed."

John grasped the man's arm. "The problem is, I don't have a while. I need it now. Five minutes ago. You can help me out, can't you, Dal?"

The man seemed torn for a minute, some internal

conflict—no doubt involving his mother—causing myriad expressions to flash across his face. Then he nodded, resolved. "You can count on me, Detective. I'll do whatever I can to assist you."

"Good," John said. "I'll be sure to note your co-operation in my report."

Dalrimple said solemnly, "Mama will be so pleased."

ZELDA'S EATERY was closed on Sundays, and normally Thea loved to sleep in. She'd never been an early riser on weekends, but in spite of her late hours the night before, she was up by seven, tiptoeing around the apartment so that she wouldn't awaken Nikki.

Mrs. Lewellyn was gone, having gotten up sometime after Thea went to bed and let herself out of the apartment. She'd been sleeping on the couch when Thea got home, and Thea hadn't had the heart to disturb her. She made a mental note to call the older woman later and thank her for coming over the evening before on such short notice. Nikki's regular baby-sitter had already made plans when Thea had called from the diner about working a double shift, but Mrs. Lewellyn had been more than willing to step in.

Back in Baltimore, Thea had never had to worry about child care. Nikki had been enrolled in a wonderful preschool, and when Thea was kept late at work, her stepmother, Mona, who was employed in the same office, was usually available to pick up Nikki. And on the rare occasions when Mona couldn't do it, Kate Ramano, Thea's best friend since high school, had readily stepped in.

Thea wondered what Kate and Mona thought of her now. She'd left Baltimore without a phone call to either of them. They had no idea where she and Nikki were, or the real story behind Rick's death, although Thea knew they'd both have their suspicions. They knew what her life had been like after the divorce—the midnight phone calls, the threats, the stalking.

Rick had made her life a living hell, and both Mona and Kate had been wonderful friends through it all. But they were human. They'd have to wonder, at times, if Rick's shooting had been self-defense or premeditated. Hadn't they heard her say, more than once, how much she wanted him dead?

Shivering, Thea poured herself a cup of coffee, then clicked on the TV, leaving the volume on mute as she surfed through the cable stations, trying to find a local news broadcast. She'd seen no sign of reporters on the scene last night, thank goodness, but she could never be too careful. The last thing she needed was to have her face splashed across newspapers. What if the Mancusos saw her picture?

For a while last night, she'd worried that Detective Gallagher might have recognized her from a wanted poster or police blotter or even a newspaper. Rick's murder, along with the disappearance of his ex-wife and daughter, was bound to have made front page in Baltimore. She couldn't be certain the story hadn't been picked up by one of the wire services and carried nationally, as well, even though she'd seen no mention of it in the past four months.

When she and Nikki had first arrived in Chicago, she'd scoured the papers and listened to news broadcasts daily, but the Windy City had its own headlines, its own problems with domestic violence.

And by the time Thea had had the nerve to venture out of their motel room and look for a newsstand carrying the *Baltimore Sun,* the whole grisly affair had been knocked from the pages by a bribery scandal involving high-ranking city officials. There'd been no mention of Rick's murder, no mention of the police corruption Thea had suspected for months.

She'd been left to imagine what the headlines must have been: VINDICTIVE EX-WIFE MURDERS DECORATED POLICE OFFICER. COP KILLER FLEES BALTIMORE WITH FOUR-YEAR-OLD DAUGHTER. STATEWIDE MANHUNT FOR COLD-BLOODED MURDERER.

Thea sometimes still had a hard time believing how much her life had changed. She'd been a business major in college and had gone to work at her father's private investigation firm right after graduation. She hadn't been interested in field work, but she had been interested in numbers. She'd run the office efficiently, cutting costs and increasing profits with her innovative ideas. Now she worked as a waitress in a diner. She'd once been a respected member of the chamber of commerce. Now she was a wanted criminal.

Deep in thought, she started violently when the doorbell sounded. Her heart skidded against her chest as her head swiveled toward the door. Who in the world would be coming to see her at this hour on a Sunday morning?

Telling herself it was probably Mrs. Lewellyn wanting to chat for a few minutes, Thea hurried to the door. But when she glanced through the peephole, she gasped in dismay.

Detective Gallagher stood in the hallway, his blue eyes so piercing she could have sworn he had the ability to look directly through the door, straight at her.

Frantically she glanced around. Was there anything incriminating in the apartment? Should she hide? Pretend she wasn't home? Grab Nikki and make a run for it?

Smoothing her hands down the sides of her chenille robe, Thea tried to get her nerves under control. There was no reason to panic. Detective Gallagher was conducting a police investigation that she had inadvertently become a part of. All she had to do was convince him that she had seen nothing last night. She had no connection to the dead woman.

But suddenly the woman's picture flashed on the TV screen, and for a moment, the smiling attractive face triggered something in Thea. Not recognition exactly, but a feeling that at sometime, somewhere, she and the dead woman's paths had crossed.

The doorbell sounded again, and casting a glance toward Nikki's bedroom, Thea patted down her tangled dark hair and pulled open the door.

Detective John Gallagher was even taller than she remembered, and more formal looking than she would have expected for a Sunday morning, unless of course, he was on his way to church. But somehow Thea doubted that. He had the appearance of a man who lived and breathed his investigations. Police work would be his religion. She knew the type all too well.

He was dressed in a dark gray suit, a starched white shirt and a silk tie that were obviously expensive—and made Thea immediately suspicious. She knew what cops made, what they had to do to afford clothing like his. A shudder of warning rippled through her.

"Good morning." His tone was cordial, but he didn't smile. His expression remained impersonal, his eyes very blue and very cold.

In spite of his grim demeanor, he was a strikingly

handsome man, Thea realized. The kind of man who almost always spelled trouble.

He gazed past her shoulder into the apartment. "May I come in? I have a few questions I need to ask you."

Dear God, what kind of questions? What in the world was he doing here? Thea frowned. "But I told you last night—I didn't see anything. I wasn't even home."

One dark brow lifted slightly. "But your little girl was, right?"

His words were like a dagger through Thea's chest. Her heart seemed to stop for a long painful moment, and she could almost feel the color draining from her face. "How did you—"

"May I come in? This won't take long."

He didn't wait for her acquiescence this time, but strode by her into the apartment, turning to face her when she remained motionless at the open doorway. Left with no option, Thea closed the door and followed him.

"Sorry to interrupt your coffee." He nodded toward the steaming mug on the cocktail table. "Smells good."

Thea merely looked at him. She had no intention of offering him coffee or anything else. This wasn't a social call, and the sooner she got rid of him, the better.

How in God's name had he known about Nikki? The Mancusos had far-reaching contacts, but still...

Thea laced her fingers together, trying to stop the trembling. She couldn't let him see how nervous she was. Couldn't give herself away. For Nikki's sake, she had to perform as she had never performed before.

"How did you know about my daughter?" She got to finish the question this time, amazed that her tone came out just right—part curiosity, part irritation at having her peaceful morning interrupted.

"We obtained a list of all the tenants in the building with children. Little girls, to be exact."

"But why?" For the first time, Thea noticed the brown paper bag he carried in one hand. Fear crept up her backbone. She lifted her gaze to meet his. "Detective Gallagher, what's this about?"

In answer, he turned toward the television. "I see you've been watching the news this morning. You probably already know that the woman who died here last night was Gail Waters. She was a reporter for a small newspaper called the *Press*."

"A reporter?" What had a reporter been doing in this building? Who had she come to see? Had she somehow found out about her and Nikki?

"The paper is local, but some of her investigative pieces also ran on a cable news channel."

Gail Waters had been on television? Was that why she'd looked familiar? Thea desperately wanted to believe that was the case. There was no reason to assume a reporter's presence in this building had anything to do with her and Nikki. And yet...

Detective Gallagher was here in her apartment, asking questions about her daughter. Obviously he thought there was a connection.

Thea lifted her chin. "As I told you last night, I don't recall having seen her before. I don't understand why you're here, Detective Gallagher."

His gaze, intent and probing, fell on her once more. "As you can imagine, there're still a lot of unanswered questions concerning her death."

"But I thought her death was a suicide. The officer

I spoke with last night said a note had been found on the body.''

"And as *I* said last night, suicide's a possibility, but we're not ruling out homicide. Not yet, at least."

"Homicide? You think someone *murdered* her?" Thea felt momentarily faint. "Who would want to kill her?" she asked weakly.

He gave her a curious look. "Reporters are a lot like cops. People sometimes don't like the questions we ask."

Thea didn't say anything to that, but she remembered the list of people Rick had claimed wanted him dead. And yet the last person he'd suspected was the one who finally did him in. Thea's stomach churned in warning. "Whether it was suicide or murder, I don't see what her death has to do with my daughter or me."

"I'm coming to that." He took something from the bag and held it up for her inspection. "Do you recognize this?"

Thea's knees almost buckled when she saw the doll. The black curls, the brown eyes, the dimpled cheeks were very much like her daughter's, which was exactly why she'd bought the doll for Nikki. It had been an extravagance they could ill afford these days, but her daughter had been so enchanted with the resemblance when they'd seen her in a shop window. Thea hadn't been able to resist. Until then, Nikki had been largely unresponsive to just about everything. The doll, named Piper after a character in Nikki's favorite book, had struck a chord deep inside the child that no one, including Thea, had been able to touch since that terrible night four months ago.

Nikki loved that doll. She would never have willingly parted with it. So how had Detective Gallagher come to be in possession of it? And what did the doll have to do with Gail Waters's death?

Chilled, Thea stared at the doll in Gallagher's hand, forcing her expression to remain placid. It was imperative that he not connect the doll to Nikki. It was crucial that the two of them remain untouched by his investigation. "You came here at this hour of the morning to ask me about a doll?" She let a trace of irritation creep into her voice.

"Do you recognize it?"

Almost absently Thea rubbed her hands up and down her arms. Detective Gallagher watched her intently, studying her as if she were a bug under his microscope. But Thea had learned a lot about bluffing from her father and from the other investigators who had worked for him. "That doll could belong to any little girl in this building. I can't imagine why you think it's my daughter's."

His eyes narrowed on her. He didn't appear fooled by her evasions. "I found this doll on the roof last night after a woman had fallen to her death. Does it, or does it not, belong to your daughter?"

On the roof! My God...

A fresh wave of fear washed over Thea, but she shook her head, denying her thoughts. This was crazy. Nikki would never have gone up to the roof. She wasn't even allowed out of the apartment without Thea's permission, and besides that, her daughter was terrified of the dark. There was no way on earth she would have gone up to that roof alone last night, and Thea couldn't imagine that Mrs. Lewellyn would have taken her.

So how had the doll gotten up there?

"You look surprised, Mrs. Lockhart. Why is that, if the doll doesn't belong to your daughter?"

Cornered, Thea chewed her lip. "The doll is a common one. I've seen it in several stores. Nikki does have one similar to it, but that doesn't mean this one is hers. It couldn't be, because there is no way she would have been on that roof. She's only four years old."

"The stairs go all the way to the roof," Detective Gallagher pointed out. "Even a four-year-old can climb stairs, and you said yourself, you were out all evening. How can you be sure your daughter wasn't on that roof?"

"Because her baby-sitter would never have allowed it." But a vision of Mrs. Lewellyn snoring peacefully on the sofa flashed through Thea's mind. Was it possible Nikki had left the apartment while the elderly woman slept? But why would Nikki do something like that? It was totally out of character for her. There was no good reason Thea could think of that would have compelled her daughter out of the apartment and up to the roof.

Either the doll wasn't hers or she'd lost it somewhere, in the hallway perhaps between here and Mrs. Lewellyn's apartment, and someone had picked it up. Someone else had taken it to the roof. That was the only possible explanation.

If only she hadn't had to work late last night. Then she would have been home with Nikki herself, and Detective Gallagher wouldn't be here asking all these questions, and she wouldn't be assailed by all these doubts. This awful premonition that somehow she and Nikki both were tied to the dead woman.

"I'm afraid I can't help you," she insisted.

Detective Gallagher stared at her for a moment

longer, then shrugged. "Sorry I wasted your time." He started for the door, but before Thea could breathe a sigh of relief, he turned back to face her. "Maybe we should ask your daughter about last night. Just to be on the safe side."

"She's sleeping, and I really don't want to wake her. She...hasn't been feeling well lately."

"I see." His eyes were dark and fathomless as his gaze rested on Thea. He looked as if he wanted to say something else, but a sound from behind her drew his attention, and Thea knew without turning that her daughter was standing in the doorway. She also knew that once Nikki saw the doll in Detective Gallagher's hand the pretense would be over.

But Piper had disappeared behind the detective's back, out of Nikki's sight. Thea thought for a moment he was actually going to leave without questioning her daughter, but then in the next instant, she told herself she should have known better. He was a cop, wasn't he? No one was sacred. Not even a wounded four-year-old girl.

"You must be Nikki." His tone lowered, became almost gentle. He walked past Thea before she could protest and knelt in front of her daughter. "Your mother and I were just talking about you. I'm Detective Gallagher."

Nikki was still dressed in her pajamas, looking soft and sweetly rumpled, her cloud of dark hair hanging in tangles down her back. She stared at Detective Gallagher, her brown eyes wide with fright.

Thea moved quickly to Nikki's side and knelt beside her, smoothing back her hair. "It's okay, sweetie. He's not going to hurt you."

She gave Gallagher a warning glance, and he smiled

reassuringly at Nikki. A rather devastating smile, Thea thought fleetingly.

"Why don't you call me John? That's what my friends call me. Some of them even call me Johnny."

How ludicrous. The man looked nothing like a Johnny.

Nikki's gaze silently probed his features, searching for signs of violence. Rick had taught their daughter well, too. Thea's heart twisted, watching her.

Still kneeling in front of Nikki, John said, "I wonder if you could help me out, Nikki. I found a pretty little doll on the roof last night. Come to think of it, she looks a lot like you. I rescued her before she got rained on, and now I'm trying to find out who she belongs to." He brought the doll around and laid her across his knee.

Nikki made a guttural sound deep in her throat and snatched Piper from his knee, clutching her tightly to her chest as she backed into the tiny hallway.

"I take it she belongs to you," John said softly. He glanced at Thea, his gaze cold and accusing. "What was your doll doing on the roof, Nikki? Did you leave her there?"

Nikki looked near tears. Her eyes were like two huge O's. She continued to back away from Detective Gallagher, until she was trapped against the wall. Then she slid down to sit on the floor, curling into a soft protective ball around Piper.

"I'm not going to hurt you," John said, making no move toward the little girl. "I just need to ask you a few questions."

Shaken by her daughter's reaction, Thea pushed past the detective and gathered Nikki into her arms. Nikki whimpered, burying her face in Thea's shoulder as she clutched Piper tightly. ''She can't answer your questions, Detective,'' Thea said coldly. ''Why don't you just go away and leave us alone?''

He rose slowly. ''I didn't come here to frighten your little girl. I'm sorry she's scared. But this is a police investigation. A woman is dead, and it's my job to find out what happened to her. If your daughter knows something—''

''She doesn't know anything. Please, she can't help you.'' Thea's arms tightened protectively around Nikki as she gazed up at Detective Gallagher, trying to appeal to the softness she'd glimpsed in him earlier, fervently hoping the compassion had been genuine. ''I don't know how her doll got on that roof, but I do know Nikki wasn't up there last night. She couldn't have been. She didn't see anything.''

''Why won't you let *her* tell me that?''

Thea drew a long trembling breath and said, almost in a whisper, ''Because she can't. She can't tell you anything. My daughter can't speak, Detective.''

JOHN STOOD at the window in Thea Lockhart's living room while he waited for her to come out of her daughter's bedroom. She'd reluctantly told him to help himself to the coffee, and he'd complied, the aroma too tempting to pass up this early in the morning. The rich steamy brew was a far cry from the lukewarm sludge at the station, and he savored the taste as he stared out the window.

The building across the street blocked the view of the lake, forcing his gaze downward. The yellow crime-scene tape had torn loose in the wind, and sometime during the night the rain had changed to snow; now a light layer of it hid the bloodstains. Passersby on the street barely gave the spot a second glance. They didn't know or didn't care that a woman had died there last night, had sucked in her last breath while plunging five stories to the ground. Had the name of her killer been on her lips when she died?

Scowling, John turned away from the window. He couldn't shake the nagging suspicion that Thea Lockhart and her daughter knew more about Gail Waters's death than they were telling. Why else was Mrs. Lockhart so nervous around him?

Mrs. Lockhart. John glanced around the apartment, taking in the shabby furniture, the basket of laundry shoved in one corner, the coloring book and crayons scattered over the dining-room table. Gold hoop earrings had been dropped into a glass bowl on the cocktail table, and a pair of white walking shoes rested near the front door.

There wasn't a trace of masculinity anywhere, including the laundry. A pink uniform lay folded on top of the basket, while the leg of a child's pajama bottom hung over one side and a lacy white bra spilled over the other.

He stared at the bra for a moment as something familiar, and unwanted, stirred in him. Meredith had been gone for some time. He was over her, and he'd long since come to terms with his failed marriage. But a woman's underthings were a reminder of the intimacy and closeness he'd once had, and he couldn't deny a certain hollowness in his life now. A loneliness he didn't often admit to.

He glanced up and caught Thea Lockhart watching him from the hallway. She knew what he'd been staring at, and a faint blush tinged her cheeks. She lifted her chin as she came into the room.

She'd changed from the chenille robe into a pair of worn jeans and navy blue sweater. Her short dark hair was combed behind her ears, but a riot of curls spilled across her forehead. She shoved it back impatiently.

"How's your daughter?" John asked, his gaze inadvertently traveling over her. She was very thin, her skin smooth and soft-looking, but she had a toughness about her, a wariness in her dark eyes that made him think she was no innocent. She'd been around. Somehow he liked that about her.

"She's playing with her doll for now, but she'll want breakfast in a few minutes."

John took the hint. He'd need to leave before then. "Why did you lie to me about the doll, Mrs. Lockhart?"

She looked surprised for a moment, as if his question had been unexpected. Then she shrugged. "I didn't lie. I wasn't sure it was Nikki's. And I still can't imagine how it got on the roof last night."

He lifted a brow as he watched her move to the tiny kitchen and pour herself another cup of coffee. She held up the pot. "Can I freshen yours?"

He shook his head. "No, thanks, I'm fine. This is good, by the way." He toasted her with his mug, and she inclined her head slightly. She didn't move back into the living room, but remained in the kitchen with the bar between them.

John left his post by the window and crossed to her. She looked vaguely startled again as he looked down at her, and she averted her gaze as she sipped her coffee.

"You still don't think your daughter left the doll on the roof?"

She frowned. "Of course I don't. You saw how shy

she is, how…easily frightened. There's no way she would have gone up to that roof alone, and I know Mrs. Lewellyn would never have taken her up there.''

''Maybe that's something we need to ask Mrs. Lewellyn.''

''I intend to,'' Thea snapped. Then, as if having second thoughts about her angry tone, she set down her coffee and gazed at him in earnest. ''Look, even if Nikki was up there—which I know she wasn't—what is it you think she can do for you? She can't tell you anything, Detective.''

John put down his own cup and leaned his arms on the bar, trying to appear relaxed and unthreatening. ''Has she always been like this?''

For a moment he thought she wouldn't answer. That same fierce protectiveness he'd witnessed earlier came over her features, and she frowned. ''No. Just since her father died.''

''I see.'' A widow. That might explain a lot, John thought, and not just the lack of male paraphernalia in the apartment. It might also explain the glimmer of desperation he'd seen in Thea Lockhart's dark eyes, and the fear. And the fact that she seemed to have a hard time looking him in the eye, acknowledging the unmistakable physical attraction that clung to their glances, their voices, the air around them. She might feel guilty about that, he decided, although there was no reason to. He didn't intend to act on his impulses and he was certain she didn't, either.

''How did her father die?'' he asked carefully.

''An accident. A…tragic accident. Nikki hasn't gotten over it yet, and I…don't like to talk about it.''

''I understand. But if there's even a slim chance that Nikki was on the roof last night, Mrs. Lockhart—''

"Thea," she said quickly. Their gazes met for a moment, and then hers darted away. She poured the rest of her coffee down the sink and rinsed out the cup. "You can call me Thea."

"That's a very pretty name."

"It's for my grandmother," she said, and then looked as if she wished she could take it back.

He smiled, trying to put her at ease. "Does your grandmother live here in Chicago?"

She almost smiled, too, as if recognizing his tactic. "My grandmother's been dead for years, Detective."

"John." When she gave him a reluctant glance, he said, "I'm named for my father, Sean."

"You're Irish?"

"Very."

"An Irish cop. That's almost a cliché, isn't it?"

"In that case, my whole family is a cliché."

John had never seen a person's demeanor change so rapidly. She'd been wary before, even a little frightened, but now her expression took on a frozen look, as if she'd donned a mask to hide her true identity, her real feelings. He'd wanted to put her at ease, but instead, her armor had grown thicker. She said stiffly, "You come from a family of cops." It wasn't a question, but a flat emotionless statement.

John shrugged. "Guilty."

"I imagine you look out for each other. Take care of each other."

John frowned at her tone. "Occasionally," he said, thinking about his brothers. Actually he would be the last person Nick would come to for help, and Tony...well, Tony was another story.

Thea said quietly, "I'd like you to go now, Detective. There's really nothing my daughter and I can do to help you.''

She was good, John realized suddenly. Too damn good. She'd distracted him from the questions he'd been intent on asking about her daughter, and all the while, convinced him he was the one in control.

He stared down at her, forcing her gaze to meet his. Her dark eyes were deep and unfathomable, a mysterious blend of fear, guile and cunning. A very dangerous mix.

''Just one more thing, *Mrs. Lockhart.*''

One brow rose slightly, and he could see that the fingers clinging to the tiny gold chain around her throat trembled. His gaze dipped, in spite of himself, to the curves beneath her sweater, and an image of that lacy white bra leaped to his mind. He could almost see her in it, her breasts straining against the fabric, his thumb stroking her through the silk—

''I know what you're thinking,'' she said hoarsely.

His gaze shot to hers. *I doubt that,* he wanted to tell her. Then again, maybe she did know. Maybe that was why the blush on her cheeks had deepened, standing out starkly against the ivory of her complexion. Her brown eyes flashed with sudden fire, and John thought absurdly that if he hadn't met her under these circumstances...if she wasn't a recent widow...if his marriage hadn't made him more than a little careful...

''You're thinking that if Nikki was on that roof, you might have an eyewitness to Gail Waters's death. It would be cut and dried. You could close your case. But you're wrong, Detective. My daughter wasn't on that roof. She couldn't have been.''

''But what if she was?'' John challenged, ignoring

the flicker of fear in her eyes. "What if Gail Waters didn't commit suicide?"

She gasped slightly, her face going paler.

"What if she was murdered and your daughter saw it all? What if she is the only one who can identify the killer? Have you thought about that, Mrs. Lockhart?"

Chapter Three

After John left Thea that morning, he drove to the county morgue, housed in the huge Chicago Technology Park off Harrison. He'd called earlier and was expected.

"What's so important about this case that I had to come in here to do the autopsy on a Sunday morning?" the assistant medical examiner demanded as she shoved a file in an already bulging drawer and slammed it shut.

John shrugged. "I figured you didn't have anything better to do. Vince is out of town, isn't he?"

Her eyes narrowed. "How did you know that?"

"Heard it through the grapevine." John wasn't about to admit to his ex-wife that he occasionally kept tabs on her new husband. Nor was he going to confide in her the possible significance of the Gail Waters case. Meredith hadn't been very supportive when his father had disappeared seven years ago. She'd suggested Sean might have been involved in something shady or even a cover-up to protect his youngest son, Tony, from suspicion in his girlfriend's brutal murder.

John had not taken kindly to Meredith's insinuations, although, if he was honest with himself, he'd have to admit the occasional doubt about his father's disappearance had crossed his own mind. Sean Gallagher wouldn't have been the first cop to go off the deep end, nor the first man to walk out on his family. He and John's mother, Maggie, had not exactly had a marriage made in heaven. And what with Tony's troubles back then…

John forced his thoughts back to the present, letting his gaze rove critically over his ex-wife. He hated to admit it, but she looked good. "So how's the baby?" he asked with only a tinge of…what? Envy? Jealousy? Self-pity?

Meredith laughed softly. She shoved back her unruly hair as she sat down at her desk. The action reminded him of Thea. They were both small women, both had dark hair, but the resemblance ended there. Meredith's skin was olive, Thea's like porcelain. Meredith could be a real bitch at times; Thea was…still a mystery.

"What can I say?" Her green eyes sparkled. "He's tiny and beautiful and absolutely wonderful. A perfect male specimen, if I do say so myself." Her gaze met John's, and for just a split second, something that might have been regret flickered in her eyes. Then she said bluntly, "You look like hell, John. What have you been doing—living at the station?"

"Lot of active cases," he muttered.

"What else is new?" She stood and pulled on a white lab coat that had been draped over the back of her chair. Her expression became sober and professional. "So what are we looking for here? Anything specific?"

"The usual. The victim took a dive off a five-story building, so I'll want to know about brain contusions." Not many lay people, including some murderers now serving prison time, knew that the bruising of the brain from a fall was different from that of a blunt-force injury. If Gail Waters had been bashed in the head before she hit the pavement, an autopsy would reveal it.

"Let's do it then," Meredith said wearily. "I've got a baby to get back to and a husband who promised to be home by dinner."

Her meaning wasn't lost on John. He'd missed more meals in the six years they'd been married than he cared to remember, and they both knew it had nothing to do with Meredith being a lousy cook. Even though she'd had her own impossible hours to deal with finishing her residency, John had been the one, more often than not, to phone with the apologies and excuses. After a while he hadn't even bothered with those.

He shouldn't have been surprised, then, when she'd announced one night that she was leaving him, nor when she'd admitted to—flung it in his face—a two-year affair with the man she was now married to. A man who had once been John's friend.

"Why should you feel so betrayed?" she'd screamed at him that night. "I'm the one who's had to put up with your mistress all these years."

"What the hell are you talking about? I've never cheated on you."

"I'm talking about that damn job of yours. You're a cop first and a man second, John. And being a husband isn't even a lousy third. I pity the next poor woman who falls in love with you."

"John?" Meredith's insistent voice brought him back to the present. She gave him a strange look. "You ready?"

"Just waiting for you." He strode toward the door

of her office. "Let's get this over with. Like you said, you've got a husband and a baby to get home to."

"And you?" Her gaze was more than a little curious.

He shrugged. "I've got a case to solve. That's what I'm good at, remember?"

"I remember you were good at a few other things, too," she said softly, her tone almost tender. "It just wasn't enough."

AFTER BREAKFAST Thea left Nikki coloring at the dining table while she went down the hall to Mrs. Lewellyn's apartment. The building, with its stained carpeting and peeling paint, was old and badly in need of refurbishing, but that was why Thea could afford the rent.

The newer lakefront high-rises on Lake Shore Drive were way out of her price range, as were the redbrick town houses cropping up near the parks. Thea had chosen the university neighborhood because of its relatively low crime rate, and because the diversity made it easier to blend in. She'd thought of everything when she and Nikki had moved in here—except the possibility of a woman being murdered in their building.

Standing in the dimly lit corridor, Thea kept an eye on her own apartment door while she waited for the elderly woman to answer hers.

When Mrs. Lewellyn finally opened the door, her eyes widened with pleasure. "Why, Thea, I didn't expect to see you this early. You got home rather late last night, didn't you, dear?" She had the barest trace of an English accent, which suited perfectly her prim-and-proper demeanor. In spite of her stooped shoulders, she was several inches taller than Thea.

"It was just after midnight," Thea said. "I want to

thank you again for coming over on such short notice to stay with Nikki.''

Mrs. Lewellyn brushed aside her gratitude. She was dressed for church, Thea noticed, in a dark blue suit and matching pumps. Her gray hair, as always, was pulled into a bun at the back of her head. ''It was my pleasure. You know I adore Nikki. She's never any trouble at all.'' She glanced past Thea into the hallway. ''Where is she?''

''She's in the apartment, coloring.'' Thea cast another glance at her door. ''I have to get back to her, but I wanted to talk to you in private for a moment.''

Mrs. Lewellyn's brows rose. ''About Nikki?''

Thea nodded. ''I need to ask you something, Mrs. Lewellyn. Did you and Nikki leave the apartment last night?''

''Leave the apartment? No, dear. Why do you ask?'' A worried light dawned in her eyes, and she put a hand to her heart. ''You heard about that poor woman who jumped off the roof last night. That's what has you so upset this morning, isn't it?''

Thea shivered. ''How did you hear about it?''

''It was on the news earlier. And I saw Mr. Dalrimple in the laundry room. Evidently the police have enlisted his help. He's strutting around like a rooster in a hen coop.''

So that was where Detective Gallagher had gotten his tenant list and how he'd known Thea had a daughter. That was also why he'd been at her door first thing this morning.

Thea told herself it was foolish to blame the building manager for her current predicament, but truth be told, she'd been uneasy about Morris Dalrimple ever since she'd moved into the building. His gaze was just a little too admiring, his tone a little too interested, and once, when she and Nikki returned from grocery shopping, Thea was almost positive she'd caught him coming out of her apartment.

He'd told her he had been knocking on her door, claiming a clause in her lease needed her initials, but Thea wasn't convinced. He'd looked guilty as she signed the paper, his face all flushed and his beady little eyes not quite able to meet hers. Thea knew he had a master key to all the apartments. What was to prevent him from coming and going as he pleased while tenants like her were at work or at school?

Shuddering, she said, ''Nikki's doll was found on the roof last night.''

''On the roof!'' Mrs. Lewellyn looked genuinely shocked and more than a little concerned. ''How on earth did it get up there?''

''I don't know.'' Thea paused. ''I was thinking that if you and Nikki *had* left the apartment last night, maybe to come over here for a few minutes, she might have dropped the doll in the hallway. Someone else could have picked it up and taken it to the roof.'' She knew she was grasping at straws, but there had to be a logical explanation. And Nikki being on the roof in the dead of night simply wasn't logical.

''I think I may know what happened,'' Mrs. Lewellyn said slowly. She wrapped a strand of pearls around her finger as she gazed pensively down the hallway. ''I'll bet you *that girl* took her up there.''

''Bliss?''

Scorn flashed in Mrs. Lewellyn's eyes, and just a hint of triumph. She didn't like Nikki's regular baby-sitter and had not been shy in voicing her opinion. *The girl's too flighty,* she'd said more than once, *And not at all reliable. You should see the kind of people who hang out in her apartment. You don't want her influence on Nikki, Thea dear. I'm more than happy to watch the child while you work.*

But as much as she appreciated Mrs. Lewellyn's help, Thea knew how trying a four-year-old could be, especially one with Nikki's problems. And Bliss was wonderful with her, so patient and loving.

"You think Bliss took the doll up to the roof?" Thea asked doubtfully.

"Why, I'm certain that must be what happened. She was very secretive when I got to your apartment last evening. She huddled with Nikki, whispering to her and laughing, and I even heard her say something about a picnic that afternoon. But when I scolded her for taking the child outside, she just fluttered those fake eyelashes at me and said something like, 'Why, Mrs. Lew, I have no idea what you're talking about. We haven't left the building all day, have we, Nikki?' She can be very disrespectful, that girl."

"So if the two of them had a picnic on the roof yesterday afternoon, Nikki could have left her doll up there then." That would explain a lot, and Thea immediately warmed to the idea.

"I'm sure of it," Mrs. Lewellyn said firmly. "Because Nikki couldn't find her doll at bedtime last night. You know how she refuses to go to sleep unless Piper is tucked in safe and sound beside her, but when I put Nikki to bed, I couldn't find the blasted doll anywhere. Nikki was very upset. I finally had to make her some warm milk, just so she'd calm down enough to drift off."

As upset as Thea was over Bliss's disobeying her orders, she was also intensely relieved. If Nikki hadn't been on the roof last night, then she couldn't have seen what happened to Gail Waters. She wasn't a witness, as Detective Gallagher had claimed, which meant she wasn't in any danger.

Unless, of course, the Mancusos found them. And Thea had no intention of letting that happen. "I'll call and ask Bliss about it when she gets home."

"She's gone off to visit her parents," Mrs. Lewellyn reminded her. "Or so she said. But that boyfriend of hers is still hanging around. I saw him on the stairs this morning. He gives me the willies, I don't mind telling you. All that long hair. That awful scruffy beard. He looks as if he hasn't bathed in weeks." She paused, shuddering delicately. "You know, if I were you, I'd really set my foot down, Thea. Bliss had no right taking Nikki up there. That roof is a dangerous place. Why, the child could have fallen off just like that poor woman—"

"I know," Thea cut in, not wanting Mrs. Lewellyn to finish her words. The visual in her mind was already too graphic. "I intend to speak to Bliss the moment she gets home."

"If you need any help with Nikki, all you have to do is ask, dear."

"Thank you."

Mrs. Lewellyn seemed reluctant to let her go, and Thea knew the old woman was probably lonely. She had no family that Thea knew of, nor any friends who came calling. Except for her church work, Mrs. Lewellyn seemed as isolated as Thea and Nikki. For a moment Thea wondered if the older woman had something in her past that she was hiding from, too.

Not likely, Thea decided as she turned down the hall to her apartment. Mrs. Lewellyn was probably just an old woman who had outlived most of her friends and family.

Something that might have been self-pity tugged at Thea's heart, and she had a vision of herself at that age, alone, bitter and still running. And what about Nikki? What kind of life had Thea sentenced her daughter to?

In a way Nikki was in her own prison. The trauma of that night, seeing her father dead on the floor, seeing the gun in her mother's hand, had sent the child running to her own dark place. A silent place.

Dr. Nevin, the child psychologist Nikki was seeing, had warned Thea that her daughter's treatment might take a long time. It could be months, even years, before Nikki trusted enough, felt safe enough, to speak. Until then, all Thea could do was be patient.

But sometimes it was so hard, seeing her daughter struggle. Thea wanted to fight Nikki's battles for her. She wanted to crawl into that cold quiet place and slay every last one of her daughter's dragons. After all, she was the one who had caused Nikki's trauma, and if she could take back that night, if she could change the course of events that had led to Rick's death, she would.

But her ex-husband would have killed her that night if she hadn't pulled the trigger on her father's gun. He might even have hurt Nikki. And that Thea could never allow.

Glancing over her shoulder, she saw that Mrs. Lewellyn had closed her door, but an uneasiness stole over her that she couldn't seem to shake. Maybe it was the thought of Rick and what she'd done, but it almost seemed as if someone was watching her. Judging her.

You're losing it, Thea scolded herself as she approached her apartment door. Sensing an invisible watcher was nothing new. Thea had long since become accustomed to glancing over her shoulder.

"You're safe," she muttered under her breath. No one was watching her. And now that she had an explanation for how Nikki's doll had gotten on the roof, she and her daughter were in the clear with the police.

Once she told Detective Gallagher what had happened, there would be no reason for their further involvement in the case. There would be no point in his coming around anymore. He would be out of their lives for good. And her and Nikki's secret would remain safe.

But as she inserted the key into the lock, a chill crawled up her backbone, and she couldn't help looking over her shoulder once more. The hallway behind her was empty, and Mrs. Lewellyn's door was still closed. No one was about.

But Thea couldn't shake the chill. She stepped quickly into her apartment and closed the door, but not all the way. She listened through a tiny crack, and almost instantly, she heard the telltale click as a door somewhere in the hall was closed.

FIRST THING Monday morning John went around to his uncle's office at the station and knocked on the open door. "You wanted to see me?"

Liam Gallagher glanced up from the report he'd been reading and motioned John into his office. Pushing sixty, Liam was still a handsome man with a shock of snow-white hair and bright blue eyes, which reflected his humor almost as often as his quick temper.

He was a seasoned detective who'd started out as a beat cop on Chicago's south side nearly forty years ago, just as his father had before him and his younger brother, Sean, had after him. Liam's son, Miles, worked in Narcotics. They were, as John had told Thea Lockhart, a family of cops.

Liam waited until John was seated, then said, "I asked Lieutenant McIntyre to send you down here because I wanted to talk to you about the report you and your partner filed yesterday morning."

"You mean the Gail Waters case?"

Liam stuck a pair of bifocals on his broad Irish nose and glanced down at the paperwork on his desk. "McIntyre said you'd requested a follow-up investigation."

"Is that a problem?"

His uncle glared at him over the rims of his glasses. "You know it is. We're short over two hundred detectives in this division, and only half the homicides in this city get solved. I don't have the time or the manpower to waste on a case that should be cleared."

"I know, I know." John sighed, all too familiar with the shortage of detectives and the stack of uncleared murder files waiting on his desk. He'd pulled a double watch for so long now he couldn't remember what it was like to get home at a decent time or have more than four or five hours of uninterrupted sleep at night. He plowed an impatient hand through his hair. "I'm not convinced Gail Waters killed herself."

"The evidence says otherwise." Liam opened the folder containing John and Roy Cox's reports and the preliminary autopsy findings. "No defense wounds, no hair, tissue or blood beneath her nails. No trace evidence or fingerprints at the scene. Toxicology tests clean. Contrecoup contusions to the brain, which means she was killed by the fall.'' He closed the folder with an unmistakable finality.

If it walks like a suicide, quacks like a suicide...

John shifted in his chair. "Look, we spent most of the day yesterday canvassing the building and interviewing the tenants. We haven't even had a chance yet to talk to her co-workers and family, let alone go through all her files. She has a database with hundreds, maybe thousands, of names from missing persons and fugitive reports she collected from every major police department in the country. One of those names could be a lead, but it'll take days to go through that list.''

"And if you don't find anything?''

John shrugged. "Then I don't. All I'm asking is for a little more time. We haven't been able to find out much about this woman except that she was a newspaper reporter. We still don't know why she was at that building on Saturday night or who she went to see.''

As John spoke, an image of Nikki Lockhart came to his mind. The little girl's dark eyes and solemn face haunted him, and he couldn't shake the notion that she might have seen something that night. Might know something she couldn't tell him.

And what about the kid's mother? What was she hiding? John didn't like to admit it, but Thea Lockhart haunted him, too. He hadn't been able to get her out of his mind all day yesterday after he'd left her, and all night last night when he'd tried to catch a few hours' sleep.

It wasn't so much that he was drawn to her, he told himself, but that he was intrigued by her. She was extraordinarily feminine with her soulful eyes and dark curly hair, but John had the distinct impression her appearance was deceiving. There was something about the way she carried herself, the fierce way she guarded her little girl that made him think she would be a formidable adversary if crossed.

"There's something else you need to know," John said hesitantly. "Something I didn't put in the report."

His uncle frowned. "What?"

John got up and closed the office door. The squad room was crowded and noisy as always, but he didn't want to take the chance his conversation might be overheard. "Gail Waters called me a few days ago and wanted to interview me for a piece she was doing on Dad's disappearance. She'd done her homework, Liam. She knew all about Ashley's murder, the frat party, Tony and Miles. She'd even been up to the prison to talk to Daniel O'Roarke on death row."

In less than a minute Liam Gallagher aged ten years. The vitality drained out of his still-muscular body, leaving him stooped, haggard and old. He slumped in his chair. "What did you tell her?"

John shrugged. "Nothing. I didn't have time to talk to her, and I didn't feel like dredging up all that old business. But…"

"But what?"

"Now she's dead."

A spark of life ignited in Liam's eyes. "What are you trying to say, Johnny?" His tone was angry

"Nothing. It may be just a coincidence. But it's a piece of the puzzle I don't think we can overlook."

"You told anybody about this? McIntyre?"

"No."

"Not even Roy Cox?"

"You're the first person I've mentioned this to." But John didn't like keeping things from his partner. He'd be madder than hell if Roy pulled something like this on him.

Liam stared at John for a long moment, then said softly, in a voice traced with an Irish accent, "You're sure about this, Johnny?"

Sure about what? That Gail Waters had called him or that she'd been murdered? "The only thing I'm sure of is that she called me and now she's dead."

Liam sat back in his chair and steepled his fingers beneath his chin. "Okay. You did the right thing bringing this to me. I'll handle it from here."

John didn't like the edge in his uncle's voice. "What are you going to do?"

Liam shrugged. "Follow procedure. There's nothing in these reports that warrant a follow-up investigation."

"I disagree."

"Let it go, Johnny." There was a warning note in his uncle's voice.

"I don't know if I can do that."

In a sudden burst of temper Liam picked up the file and flung it at John. The contents spilled over his desk. "That wasn't a request, goddamn it, that was an order." His blue eyes glittering with fire, he folded his arms on his desk and leaned toward John. "You've always been a good cop, Johnny, and one helluva detective, but sometimes you remind me too much of Sean. You don't know when to let go. You gotta think about this one, son. You gotta think what it would do to the family if you started asking the wrong questions. Think about your brother. Ashley's murder nearly did Tony in back then. Look what it's done to his life. I've had to appear before more review boards on his behalf than I care to remember. The kid's always been hanging on by a thread. What do you think would happen to him if he had to relive all that?''

"Tony's got a few problems," John admitted. "But he's also a cop, a damn good one when he chooses to be. He'd be the last person to condone a cover-up."

"Cover-up?" Liam took off his glasses and rubbed his eyes. "I'd be careful how I used that word if I were you. Makes the brass mighty nervous. I shouldn't have to remind you, you'd be stepping on some pretty big toes if you tried to pursue this angle."

"You mean Dawson?"

"He's never gotten over his stepdaughter's death. She was like his own child. He was crazy about her. If you start trying to connect some two-bit reporter's suicide to Ashley's murder and Sean's disappearance, Dawson's not gonna like it one bit."

John knew that was true. Everyone generally regarded Superintendent Ed Dawson as a fair man, but he could be ruthless when it came to guarding his family's privacy. John's brother Tony and his cousin Miles had both sworn they'd seen Dawson's son, Eddie, at the frat party that night, but somehow that part of their statements had never made it into the official report.

"What if Gail Waters talked to Dawson, too?" John asked quietly.

Liam stared at him for another long moment, then got up and strode to the dirty window. Shoving his hands in his pockets, he gazed out at the bleak morning, but John doubted his uncle was counting the snow flurries. It was strange to think that the events of seven years ago were still causing so many people so much anguish.

"I've been over the what-ifs in that case a thousand times. What if I'd made Miles stay home that night?

What if Sean had kept Tony on a shorter leash? What if he and Ashley hadn't gotten so serious that year? What if Daniel O'Roarke had stayed on his own side of town...?''

His words trailed off and John said, "What if Dad hadn't started thinking Daniel might be innocent."

The quiet words were like gunshots. Liam turned from the window, his face a mask of pain. "Don't ever say that again. Don't even think it."

"But it's true, isn't it? Dad was having doubts about his own arrest."

"You don't know what the hell you're talking about, Johnny. You're starting to sound like Tony."

John let that one pass. "He was starting to have doubts and then he disappeared."

Liam's voice hardened. "The O'Roarkes killed Sean. You know that as well as I do."

"I know that his body was never found. I know that we've never been able to prove anything."

"We've never been able to prove a lot of things on the O'Roarkes, but that doesn't mean they're not guilty as hell. If you're starting to think one of the O'Roarkes is innocent, then God help you."

"I'm not thinking that," John said wearily. "All I'm saying is that this connection with Gail Waters and Dad's disappearance troubles me. I'd like to check into it. I'd like to find out what other stories she might have been working on when she died. What other disappearances she might have been investigating. Maybe that's why she was at that building Saturday night. Maybe someone there can shed some light on all this for us."

Liam drew a long breath and released it as he turned

back to the window. "Why do I get the feeling you're going to move on this thing regardless of what I say?"

"Because you know, as well as I do, this case smells."

"Give me one good reason why I should let you do this," Liam said grimly.

"Because," John said, staring at his uncle's profile, "I may have a witness."

Chapter Four

By the time Thea's shift ended at three Monday afternoon, she was more than ready to get off her feet. She'd started working at the diner three months ago in hopes of keeping a low profile, and during that time, she'd gained new respect for waiters and waitresses. Today, her back ached, her head throbbed and she generally felt lousy.

She knew the stress she'd been under for months was having an adverse effect on her health. And her run-in with the police Saturday night and early Sunday morning certainly hadn't helped the situation. She hadn't slept well for the past two nights, and the strain was wearing on her nerves. It was time to take action.

With that in mind, she'd put in a call to Detective Gallagher on her break that morning to try to convince him that Nikki had left her doll on the roof on Saturday afternoon—hours before Gail Waters had died. There was no way her daughter could have seen anything.

But Detective Gallagher had been out, so she'd spoken to his partner, instead. Which had been a relief in a way, she reflected as she picked up Nikki at her preschool on Dorchester. The less she had to deal with Detective Gallagher—John, as he'd told her to call him—the better. Under the circumstances, she wouldn't feel comfortable in the company of any police officer, but John Gallagher was just so…intense.

And handsome, a little voice taunted her.

Yes, that, too, she acknowledged. But Rick had been good-looking, too, with his Italian heritage and gregarious personality. She knew better than anyone how deceiving looks could be.

Thea had never considered herself naive. Her father, a successful private investigator and a very smart man, had raised her to be street savvy. Working in his office, she had learned she had an instinct for liars. She'd known when clients weren't telling the truth, and yet Rick Mancuso had wormed his way into her life so deftly, so cunningly, that she'd been trapped in his web before her first suspicion ever surfaced.

Over the years she'd tried to convince herself that her vulnerability following her father's murder had been her downfall. Her grief and rage had blinded her to Rick's true nature.

He'd been the detective assigned to her father's case, and the moment Thea had set eyes on him, she'd known he would find the killer. In spite of the courteous, almost deferential way he'd addressed her and her stepmother, his eyes had been hard and coldly determined. There might even have been a hint of cruelty that, at that particular moment, had appealed to Thea. She'd wanted him to be ruthless. She'd wanted him to hunt down her father's murderer with a vengeance. And when Rick had done exactly that, Thea had convinced herself she was in love with him.

It had only taken her a few months to realize what a terrible mistake she'd made, but by then it was too late. She was already pregnant by the time she'd learned, the hard way, that the cruelty she'd glimpsed in Rick's eyes wasn't reserved only for the murderers he relentlessly hunted. It was for anyone who got in his way. Including her.

And the truly frightening part was he could get away with it. He was from a family of powerful cops. Cousins, brothers and uncles who would say and do anything to back one another up. Even lie in a court of law and threaten witnesses.

One by one the Mancusos, as well as Rick's friends in the Baltimore Police Department, had taken the stand against Thea in her custody battle for Nikki shortly after her daughter's birth. They'd told lie upon lie about Thea's fitness as a mother, about her faithfulness as a wife.

But the person who had done the most damage was Rick's mother. Lenore Mancuso had lied with impunity, weeping bitter beguiling tears as she'd pleaded with the judge and jury not to deliver her sweet little granddaughter into the hands of such an evil vicious woman.

Their lies and manipulations had almost cost Thea her daughter. She and her lawyer had finally prevailed, but it wasn't likely she could do so again. If the Mancusos found her now...

It was possible, of course, that her stepmother, who still worked for the firm Thea's father had founded, might employ their own detectives to track down her and Nikki. But Thea didn't think that was the case. Mona would know the danger, the risk in leading the Mancusos to her.

She suppressed a shudder as she helped Nikki bundle up before leaving the school building. She loved her daughter so much, but every time she looked into those dark eyes, she couldn't help remembering that terrible night...what she'd done...

Pausing long enough to gather up Nikki's work from the day and to say goodbye to her teacher, Thea followed her daughter through the door. Nikki kept her hand in Thea's as they trudged down the wet sidewalk, content to be led along the street. But when they got to the entrance of a small park, she stopped and gazed longingly at the playground behind the wrought-iron gate. In spite of the cold and wind, she still loved being outside. It was a kind of freedom, Thea suspected, and she tried to humor her daughter whenever possible, even on frigid days like today.

But whereas most children Nikki's age would have been laughing, running, flapping their arms like birds, spinning round and round until they grew dizzy and collapsed to the ground, Nikki walked slowly toward the swings, climbed into one of the seats and pushed herself gently to and fro as she gazed off into the distance.

What was she thinking? Thea wondered, her throat tight. Was she remembering that night? Was she blaming her mother for taking away her father?

"Looks like we may get some serious snow tonight," a deep voice said beside her.

Thea jumped, dropping the drawings she'd been clutching. The wind whipped the papers into a frenzy, and before Thea had time to react, John Gallagher bent and deftly retrieved the pages in swift economical motions.

Thea accepted them, glad that her gloves prevented accidental contact with his skin. She wasn't sure why, but there was something disturbing about his large hands, something masculine and overtly sexy.

She turned back to watch her daughter as he sat down on the bench beside her. "Mind if I join you?"

She frowned. "How did you know I was here?"

"I got your message from my partner. I decided to drop by and talk to Mrs. Lewellyn myself. She told me you and Nikki sometimes come to the park after you pick her up from school."

Thank you, Mrs. Lewellyn, Thea thought not kindly. She adjusted her stocking cap more snugly. The wind made her ears ache. John didn't wear anything on his head, and she wondered absently how he stood the cold.

"Why did you need to see me again? I told Detective Cox about the doll and how it got on the roof. That explains everything, doesn't it?"

He hesitated. She could feel his gaze on her, but she refused to face him. Her heart thudded against her chest, but she told herself it was because his sudden appearance had been such a shock. She'd thought— hoped and prayed—she'd seen the last of him.

"It makes sense," he said. "But I'd still like to talk to the baby-sitter, this Bliss Kyler you told Detective Cox about."

Thea had wanted to talk to Bliss, too, but unfortunately the girl had gotten to the apartment so late this morning that Thea hadn't had time to question her. She'd had to rush off to work, and the diner had been so busy she hadn't had a chance to phone home until eight-thirty. By then, Bliss had already left to walk Nikki to school. Afterward Bliss headed off to her own classes at the university. Rather than trying to track her down, Thea had decided to go by Bliss's apartment tonight.

However, she didn't relish doing so with John Gallagher in tow. What if Bliss didn't corroborate the story? John's suspicions would continue to grow, and Thea would have no choice. She and Nikki would have to run again.

Thea suddenly felt wearier than she could ever remember. *Why can't you just go away and leave us alone?* she silently pleaded. But when she finally turned to meet his gaze, her heart sank. The determination in his eyes was all too familiar, along with a flicker of something she fervently hoped was not cruelty.

"Bliss will tell you the same thing Mrs. Lewellyn told you." Thea's voice held far more conviction than she felt. "Nikki was nowhere near that roof on Saturday night."

"I hope you're right," he said softly. His blue eyes seemed to darken as he stared at her, and Thea's heart fluttered in warning.

She could tell he was attracted to her, and the feeling was far from one-sided. He was very good-looking, tall and broad-shouldered, with an air of confidence that wasn't arrogant or smug, but rather a poise that came from years of self-reliance. He was a man comfortable with his own capabilities, which, Thea had no doubt, were considerable.

She shivered as their gazes clung for a moment and an electrical current seemed to flow between them. A warm blush spread upward from her chest to her cheeks, but before she could turn away, John glanced toward the playground, severing the connection.

Thea felt oddly disappointed. It had been nearly four years since her divorce, four years since she'd felt anything but suspicion and a fair amount of contempt for a man like John Gallagher. He'd told her, as plainly as if he'd spoken the words aloud, that, yes, he found her attractive. Yes, there was a definite spark between them, but he wasn't going to do anything about it. She was off-limits as far as he was concerned.

She tried to bolster her relief by letting her own gaze drift to her daughter and reminding herself that her and Nikki's safety depended on their anonymity. John Gallagher was the last man on earth she should get involved with.

As if sensing her mother's scrutiny, Nikki left the swing and started toward her. When she drew even with the slide, she stopped for a moment, her gaze climbing the steps almost reverently.

Beside the equipment, Nikki looked tiny and defenseless, and Thea's heart ached for her daughter all over again. Nikki had always been a shy introverted child, but since that night, she'd developed several phobias for which Dr. Nevin said the only cure was patience, love and a secure environment.

Luckily Thea had the first two qualities in abundance where her daughter was concerned. And she would do almost anything to ensure the third.

Nikki came to stand beside Thea, resting her red-gloved hand on her mother's knee as she looked warily at John.

"Do you remember Detective Gallagher?" Thea asked her.

"Hi, Nikki. How's your doll doing after her night on the roof?"

When Nikki showed no reaction, he said easily, "You like coming to the park?" He didn't seem in the least fazed by her lack of response. He was actually quite good with the child, which surprised Thea. Yesterday she'd thought him cold and distant.

He leaned forward slightly, talking to Nikki. "When I was a kid, my brothers and I used to play in a park not far from here. My sister, too, sometimes, although she was younger than the rest of us. You kind of remind me of her, except she has red hair. Her name is Fiona. She's all grown up now."

Thea was tempted to ask him how many brothers and sisters he had, but she didn't want to get too personal. She didn't want him to think she was interested in any aspect of his life.

He glanced at the playground. "I always liked the swings the best. How about you?" He turned back to Nikki. When she still didn't respond, he said, "Ever go down the slide?"

So he'd noticed her interest in the slide, too. Thea held her breath. Nikki remained motionless and emotionless.

"When I was about your age, I hated the slide." John grimaced. "I didn't like climbing those steps and looking down at the ground. But there was this one time when I managed to make it all the way to the top. Know what happened?"

Nikki's little face was almost swallowed by the scarlet hood of her parka. She lifted her finger and scratched the side of her nose, but Thea could tell her daughter wasn't bored. She was hanging on every word John said, and it occurred to Thea, almost with surprise, that her daughter had never been around men much. Rick had come by only when it suited him, and that had been too often in Thea's opinion. He hadn't known the first thing about communicating with a child, especially one as shy as Nikki. Thea was convinced the only reason he'd ever wanted custody was because he'd known how badly it would hurt her. And perhaps because his mother had urged him on.

"I got stuck," John said.

Thea glanced at him, half surprised, half amused. "How did you get stuck on a slide?" she asked doubtfully.

"My jeans got caught on a bolt. I couldn't get them loose. None of the other kids could, either. I had to sit way up on top of that slide until one of the older boys came up to rescue me."

Nikki had edged a little closer to John. She was leaning her forearms on Thea's knee as she gazed at him raptly.

"He had to cut my jeans loose with a pocketknife. I had a big hole in the seat of my pants. I told everyone that was the reason I wouldn't come down, but truth was, I was just plain scared. So I sat up there until it got dark and everyone else went home."

Nikki turned and glanced at the slide.

"Know how I finally got down?"

She shook her head almost imperceptibly.

"My grandfather came and got me. He was this great big giant of a guy with a deep gruff voice that had always scared the daylights out of me before. He climbed the steps two at a time and stood at the top, staring down at me. He said, 'Johnny, this slide is a lot like life. You go up, you come down, and then you go back up again. See that bump in the middle? That's like real life, too. It's fun and scary at the same time. Now you can sit up here avoiding those bumps, or you can go down this slide, have a few laughs, maybe land on your rear a time or two, but then you get right back up and go do it all over again. That's what makes life worth living.'''

John told the story in a thick Irish accent, and Thea could almost picture a white-haired man with laughing blue eyes. An older version of John. With a pang she realized that Nikki would never know what it was like to have a grandfather to come to her rescue. To dote on her. To think the sun rose and set on her.

Tears suddenly stung Thea's eyes. She told herself it was foolish to get misty over a corny childhood story, but she couldn't help comparing John Gallagher to Rick. They were both cops, both very determined men, but Rick would never have admitted to a weakness like that. In fact, he would have carried Nikki, kicking and screaming, up the slide and forced her to go down. Nikki's sensitivity—what he'd perceived as weakness—had always provoked him.

"I learned a pretty good lesson that day." He paused, glancing at Thea. "Life is full of bumps, some a little scarier than others. But if you get stuck on one, you shouldn't be afraid to ask for help."

Was that a message for her daughter or for her? Thea wondered uneasily. "Sounds like you come from a big family," she heard herself murmur.

"Two brothers and a sister, lots of cousins, aunts and uncles."

"All of them cops?" she couldn't help asking.

John shrugged. "My brothers are, and my father was."

"Was?"

"He's…dead." A shadow crossed his features and he glanced away.

"I'm sorry," she said. "I know what it's like to lose a parent. My mother died when I was little. It was just my father and me for years, and then he remarried about a year before he died." *That's way more than he needs to know,* Thea scolded herself. But her father had told her once that the trick of working undercover was to rely on the truth as much as possible. She shrugged. "Now it's just Nikki and me."

"What about her father's family?"

The question was softly spoken, not like an interrogation at all—but that was what made it so scary. Thea hadn't seen it coming and she should have. She was her father's daughter, for God's sake. She should have recognized a trap long before it was sprung, but John Gallagher was good. He'd made her want to open up to him, and that was a very dangerous thing.

"There's no one," she said coolly. She rose and took her daughter's gloved hand in hers. "It's getting late. I have to get home and fix Nikki her dinner."

John stood and glanced at his watch. "It is late," he agreed almost absently. "Later than I thought, and I've suddenly realized I skipped lunch today. There's a pizza place not far from here. I think they may even serve hot chocolate."

Thea's heart started to pound. That she was even momentarily tempted by his invitation proved how truly dangerous he was. But she could almost smell the succulent aroma of a Chicago pan pizza, taste the spices and sauces and cheese; the luxury of having someone wait on her for a change was almost impossible to resist.

She and Nikki rarely ate out, even inexpensive takeout. Her earnings at the diner didn't even cover the necessities, let alone frivolous treats like pizza. Luckily she had her savings, her stash, as she thought of it, to supplement her income and pay for Nikki's sessions with Dr. Nevin.

Her father had left her quite a bit of money when he

died, and Thea had added to it regularly ever since her divorce, because she'd known there might come a time when she'd need to leave town quickly and quietly with Nikki.

No one, not even her stepmother, had known about her stash, nor of the false IDs and passports one of her father's associates had supplied her with. Those preparations would make her look even guiltier if she was caught. There wasn't a jury in Baltimore who would believe Rick's death wasn't premeditated. His family and friends would make sure of that.

"How about it?" John urged quietly. "You two up for pizza?"

Thea said just as quietly, "I know what you're doing."

One dark brow rose in question.

She gave him a direct unwavering glare. "All that talk about the park, the slide, your brothers and sister. And now pizza. You're pushing all the right buttons, aren't you, Detective? You're trying to use my daughter, ingratiate yourself with her to try and solve your case, and I won't have it."

His gaze was unfathomable. Thea had no idea what he was thinking. "Whether you believe it or not, I only have Nikki's best interests at heart. I'm not convinced Gail Waters's death was a suicide. I'm still not convinced your daughter didn't see something that night. I'm worried about her safety…Thea."

Her name on his lips sent a shiver of something she didn't want to name up her backbone, made her heart flutter in awareness. She hadn't been attracted to a man in years. She'd been too busy building a career, taking care of her daughter and trying to keep her ex-husband and his family off her back. And now, suddenly, at the worst possible time, with the worst possible man, she was feeling things she had no business feeling. Wanting things that were as far out of her reach as the moon.

"Why can't you just go away and leave us alone?" she whispered.

His gaze softened, touched her lips, and Thea trembled, clutching her daughter's hand as if Nikki was her only lifeline. And maybe she was. Maybe her daughter was the only thing that would keep her sane through this.

"I'd like to help you," he said.

"We don't need your help." Still gripping Nikki's hand, Thea turned toward the street.

Behind her John said, "What are you so afraid of?"

Thea didn't respond, just kept walking. She prayed he wouldn't follow, but after a moment he caught up with them, slowing his long stride to match hers and Nikki's. She swore under her breath. How on earth was she going to get rid of him?

"I'm sorry. I'm not trying to harass you," he said, but he didn't sound the least bit sorry. And why should he? He'd reason he was just doing his job, Thea thought bitterly. "I'm not trying to use Nikki. I'm worried about her. I'm worried about both of you."

"We can take care of ourselves." *My God, if you only knew what I've done to keep my daughter safe. And I'd do it again if I had to.*

"I'm sure you can under normal circumstances." His dark hair glistened with moisture from the snow flurries. "But there're some things about this case you may not be aware of."

"What are you talking about?" She stopped and looked up at him. He towered over her. Thea had never been as conscious of her diminutive stature as she was at that moment. And as if to prove her own strength, she bent and picked up Nikki, keeping her between them.

Now who's using your daughter? a little voice taunted her.

John gazed down at them, his face a mask Thea couldn't decipher. "Have dinner with me and we'll talk about it," he said.

Thea frowned. "I don't think that's a good idea."

"Why not?" Before giving her time to answer, he said to Nikki, "What kind of pizza do you like? Sausage? Pepperoni? I'm partial to just plain cheese myself."

No fair. Cheese was every kid's favorite.

Nikki looked at Thea, her expression almost hopeful. The fact that her daughter showed such a reaction at all was a positive sign, but did a miracle, even so small a one, have to be here, now, with John Gallagher?

"Don't tell me you're not using my daughter now," she accused.

John shrugged. "I wasn't going to. Here, let me." He took Nikki from her arms before Thea could protest. And to her surprise, her daughter went with very little resistance.

What on earth was going on here? Thea wondered in near panic. Nikki had always been wary of strangers, even before Rick's death. It took her a long time to warm up to people, but she looked almost...relaxed in John's arms and way too secure.

She hadn't learned yet, as Thea had, that a man like John Gallagher almost always had an ulterior motive for his kindness.

"So you don't have any family in Chicago?"

They'd finished a large pizza—half cheese and half

sausage—in an alarmingly short period of time. Thea was a delicate-looking woman, but she wasn't all that delicate when it came to eating, he'd discovered. She'd almost kept pace with him, consuming two large slices and relishing every bite. It made him wonder what other appetites she might have.

They were sitting across the table from each other, he with a beer and she with a glass of wine while Nikki finished her hot chocolate. Thea had seemed to relax over dinner, but the moment he asked her a personal question, he saw her tense.

Her gaze shot to Nikki, who seemed oblivious to the babble of voices all around her. The place was crowded with rowdy children and tired parents trying to unwind after a hard day's work. Thea leaned toward him, lowering her voice so her daughter wouldn't overhear. "I thought we were going to talk about the Gail Waters case. You said there was something about it I didn't know, Detective—"

"John," he reminded her.

"John..." She faltered over his name, glancing up at him and then away.

He decided to come to her rescue. "She was a reporter who investigated unsolved disappearances and cases involving missing persons and fugitives. She aired some of the pieces on a local cable show called *Vanished!*"

John wasn't sure if it was the harsh lighting in the restaurant or his imagination, but Thea's face seemed to pale all of a sudden, and she couldn't quite meet his eyes.

"I didn't know that," she said softly. "Nikki and I don't watch much television."

He nodded, wondering about her reaction. She was okay now, but for just an instant, before she looked away, he could have sworn he saw fear in her eyes. He leaned toward her over the table. Nikki was busy using the crayon on a paper place mat the waitress had given her earlier. With her fist closed tightly around the crayon, she drew dark red streaks through the fairy-tale characters on the mat.

Like Thea, he lowered his voice so that Nikki couldn't hear him. "I think she may have been investigating someone in your building."

A frown flitted across Thea's brow, but other than that, her expression was implacable. "Why do you think so?"

"Because that's what she did for a living. She went to that building to see someone. Someone inside had to have let her in."

"Not necessarily. She could have followed one of the tenants inside. It happens a lot."

"Yeah, it does," John agreed. "But that still doesn't explain what she was doing there. Why no one has come forward to say he or she saw her that night. She didn't just pick that building at random to jump off. It doesn't work that way."

"I guess not." Thea's voice sounded a little strained. She rubbed a hand across her brow as if she was very weary. She still had on her uniform from the diner, and John knew she'd probably been on her feet for hours. He was suddenly glad he'd brought her and Nikki out for pizza tonight, that the glass of wine she'd sipped all through dinner had brought at least a momentary glow to her otherwise pale complexion. "I still don't understand what any of this has to do with Nikki and me. I explained to you about the doll. What more do you want from us?''

He glanced at Nikki again. Her dark head was bowed over her coloring. He wasn't sure if she was very adept at tuning out her surroundings, or if she was very adept at pretending to. He kept his voice lowered just in case. ''I could use your help.''

Her frown deepened. ''I don't understand.''

''I have a feeling Saturday night wasn't the first time Gail Waters went to your building. I want you to think back, try to remember whether you may have seen her there before. Who she might have been talking to.''

''I told you before I didn't recognize her.'' But even as she said the words, something that might have been alarm flickered in her eyes. She hid it almost immediately. ''Why me, Detective? There're dozens of tenants in that building. What makes you think I'm the only one who can help you?''

''It's a wild shot,'' he admitted. But there was something about Thea Lockhart that didn't quite ring true. She knew more than she was telling, he'd lay a bet on it.

She leaned across the table, pinning him with an accusing glare. ''You said earlier you didn't want to harass us, but I think you're getting dangerously close. I told you I didn't recognize the victim. I explained to you about Nikki's doll. I don't know what more you want from us, but I'd like to think this is the end of it, Detective.'' She grabbed up her and Nikki's coats and gloves, and struggled out of the booth. ''Come on, sweetie. Time to go home.''

Nikki glanced up, her dark eyes round and solemn. John had a feeling she hadn't missed as much of their conversation as they would have liked. She crawled out of the booth and waited for her mother to help her on with her coat.

John threw some bills on the table and followed them through the noisy restaurant. He caught up with Thea at the door and took her arm. "I'm not going to apologize for doing my job."

"I don't expect you to. I just want you to leave my little girl and me alone. Let us get on with our lives."

"And if Gail Waters *was* murdered?"

She challenged his gaze. "It has nothing to do with us."

"I wish I could believe that," he murmured as he followed Thea and Nikki out of the restaurant.

WHEN JOHN HAD TOLD HER that Gail Waters investigated cases involving missing persons and fugitives, Thea's heart had leaped to her throat and remained there. She'd used every ounce of her willpower not to react, but the information had blindsided her.

Why hadn't she known about this before? She'd seen the accounts of Gail Waters's death on the news, but they'd only said she was a local newspaper reporter and TV producer. They'd said nothing about missing persons and fugitives. They'd said nothing about a show called *Vanished!*

If Thea had known this earlier…

Dear God, it was so obvious why Gail Waters had come to this building. She'd come to investigate Thea and Nikki. Who else could it be? The chances that one of the other tenants was also in hiding were slight.

No, she and her daughter had undoubtedly been Gail Waters's target. And it was only a matter of time before John Gallagher figured that out for himself. If he hadn't already.

But…who had let Gail into the building? And why had she gone up to the roof and thrown herself off without ever having spoken to her?

Or had someone pushed her, as John suspected? Someone trying to protect Thea and Nikki?

Another thought occurred to her. If she and Nikki had been the target of Gail Waters's investigation, then the reporter would have files and notes somewhere that she'd compiled on the case, evidence that would link Thea to Rick's death. But just as frightening, if Gail had been on to her, it would give Thea a motive for wanting her dead. The moment the police found something to link her to the dead woman, Thea would become their number-one suspect.

She trembled violently as she unlocked the front door of her building. John waited out front in his car until they were safely inside, and then she reluctantly waved to him. Turning quickly from the glass door, she and Nikki hurried up the stairs. As they neared the top, a man was just starting down.

He wore a dark heavy overcoat with the collar turned up, and as he moved aside to allow them to pass, his gaze touched Thea's briefly. A chill raced up her backbone. For a moment she thought he was John. She even started to call his name, but then she realized she had just seen him drive off. There was no way he could have parked his car and beat them up here.

Uneasy, Thea glanced back over her shoulder. As the man stepped onto the landing, he looked back up at her. There was something in his eyes, a cold familiarity that made her heart almost stop.

He looked enough like John Gallagher to be his brother.

Chapter Five

That night, Thea tried to relax around Nikki. She didn't want her own nerves and fears causing her little girl even more anxiety, but her conversation with John had left her badly shaken. Not only could her past come out, but she could also be charged with Gail Waters's murder. It was almost too terrifying to contemplate, but she had to think about it. She had to consider every angle of the situation and try to figure a way out.

When the doorbell rang shortly after she'd put Nikki to bed, she was almost glad for the distraction. After glancing in the peephole, she opened the door.

Mrs. Lewellyn stood in the hallway, her face puckered with worry. "I'm so sorry to disturb you, Thea, dear, but may I come in for a moment? I need to speak with you."

"Of course." Thea stepped back to let the woman enter, then closed and locked the door behind her. "Would you like some coffee? A cup of tea?"

"No, thank you. I won't trouble you."

"Please sit down." Thea motioned to the sofa. "What's wrong? Has something happened?"

"I'm afraid so." Mrs. Lewellyn's mouth looked

pinched around the edges. "A police detective was here earlier. He was asking a lot of questions."

Thea's heart skipped a beat. "About Nikki's doll being on the roof?"

Mrs. Lewellyn nodded. "He was very persistent. I told him about Bliss and the picnic and what you and I suspect, but I'm not sure he was convinced."

"What was the detective's name?"

"I can't quite remember. It was an Irish name," she said with faint disapproval.

"John Gallagher?"

"Gallagher." Mrs. Lewellyn's eyes narrowed as she thought. "Yes, I believe that was it. Like I said, he came by this afternoon and then returned a little later. When I saw who it was the second time, I pretended I wasn't home. I didn't want to let him in again."

Thea thought about the man she and Nikki had seen on the stairs, the one who had reminded her of John. Could that man be one of John's brothers? Did John have his whole family working on the case?

Mrs. Lewellyn's hand fluttered to her chest. "I don't mind telling you, he frightened me a little. There was something…unsettling about him, and all those questions he kept asking about you and Nikki—"

"What about us?" Thea cut in sharply. "What else did he ask you?"

"How long you've lived here, where you're from, if you have friends and family who come to visit you…"

"Oh, no," Thea whispered, her heart plunging. It was starting already. The questions and suspicions. Next would come a full-scale investigation.

Her hand rose to her throat. She was already starting to feel cornered.

"Now don't you worry. I didn't tell him anything,"

Mrs. Lewellyn said quickly. She looked quite proud of herself. "Just the story you and I agreed on about the doll."

She made it sound as though they'd hatched a scheme together. Thea frowned. "It wasn't a story. As far as we know, it's the truth."

"Yes, yes, of course. Now if Bliss will just be co-operative, and Mr. Dalrimple can keep his mouth shut—"

"What does Mr. Dalrimple have to do with this?"

"I told you, he thinks he's part of the investigation. He says the police have enlisted his help, and now he thinks he has the right to go prying into other people's business." She paused, gathering her indignation. "You know he has an eye for you, Thea, dear."

Unfortunately Thea had suspected as much. "I'm sure he means well."

"Yes, well, ax murderers sometimes claim they have good intentions, but their victims are still just as dead. I'm only giving you this advice because I've grown so fond of you and Nikki. You're like family to me. Watch out for that man, Thea. I don't care at all for the way he looks at you."

"I'll be careful."

"You do that. There's something almost sinister about that little man. He's always very quick to speak so lovingly of his mother, but how long has it been since you've seen her?"

"I've never seen her," Thea said.

"Exactly."

"You're not implying Mr. Dalrimple—"

"I'm not implying anything," Mrs. Lewellyn said primly. "But I see and hear a lot of things around this building, and what I'm seeing and hearing lately disturbs me a great deal.'' She gave Thea an enigmatic look. ''That reporter came here for a reason, you know. She came here to see someone.''

''Do you know who?'' Thea asked shakily. Something about Mrs. Lewellyn's demeanor troubled her tonight. There was a strange glimmer in her eyes, and Thea found herself wondering again about the older woman's background.

As if reading Thea's mind, she said cagily, ''Well, that's what the police are supposed to find out, isn't it, dear? But they'll be all too quick to call it a suicide, you mark my words. That's how they operate. Unless, of course, someone raises a stink about it, in which case they'll be looking for someone to pin the blame on.''

''Meaning?''

Mrs. Lewellyn's eyes were bright and knowing as she gazed at Thea. ''Meaning you'd better get yourself over to Bliss's apartment and find out what she knows about Nikki's doll being on that roof. We'd all better get our stories straight before Detective Gallagher comes snooping around here again.''

JOHN SPENT THE EVENING going through the police report on his father's disappearance, although he knew almost everything in the file by heart. He'd broken department protocol years ago by copying portions that were still restricted, and as he thumbed through the forbidden pages, he wondered briefly what his brothers, especially Nick, would think if they knew of his transgression. Nick had accused John once of caring more about rules than he did about the truth.

''You know what your problem is?'' he'd said.

''You see everything in black and white, John. There are no shades of gray in your book.''

Ever since their father's disappearance, Nick, the middle brother, had carried a huge chip on his shoulder regarding John. As the eldest son, John had tried to step in and take care of the family, be there if and when they needed him, but Nick had never wanted any part of his help.

The situation had worsened when John had once let slip his secret doubt that their father was really dead, that he might have just up and left because of the pressure he was under during the Ashley Dallas investigation, and maybe because of his deteriorating marriage.

John and Nick had actually come to blows over that. Nick had always been a hothead, and he'd poured every ounce of his frustration and grief, every kernel of his hatred for the O'Roarkes, whom he swore were responsible for their father's death, into his rage against John. Nick had wanted to kill him that day. John had no doubt about that. If their mother hadn't stepped in and separated them, he wasn't sure how far the fight would have gone.

That had been seven years ago, just months after their father's disappearance, and Nick's resentment of John hadn't lessened over the years. If anything, it had grown stronger, just as his hatred for the O'Roarkes had.

Getting up to fetch himself a beer, John glanced out the kitchen window of his south-side bungalow. Cassandra rubbed against his leg, and he bent automatically to pick her up. He stood smoothing the cat's soft fur as he stared out into the frozen night.

His house was on a corner and the window faced a

dead-end street. For a moment he thought he saw someone moving stealthily among the cars parked at the curb, but as John watched, the figure brazenly moved under the streetlight. He was bundled up against the cold, his head covered, his face shielded by a scarf. The man's gaze seemed to touch John's for just a brief instant through the window before he turned and headed down the sidewalk.

Was it Fischer? John didn't like the idea of the informant knowing where he lived. He knew nothing about the man, other than he seemed to have an eerie ability to feed John the right information at the right time. In fact, he'd helped him solve three murder cases in the past year, but there was something about the man that disturbed him. Fischer always made contact at night, and he always took care that John never saw his face, which in itself wasn't all that unusual for a police informant. They often lived in a shadow world. What bothered John about the man was something intangible. Something that made the hair on the back of his neck stand on end when they talked.

John's first inclination now was to go charging after the man, see if he was indeed Fischer and find out what he was up to, what he might know about the Gail Waters case. But John knew from past experience that Fischer wouldn't talk until he was ready. He wouldn't be found, either, unless he wanted to be.

John set Cassandra on the floor, and the Persian meowed her protest. ''You know what your problem is?'' he muttered. ''You want me when you want me. The rest of the time I'm just a meal ticket.''

Miffed that he hadn't fallen for her ploy, Cassandra stretched, making sure to dig her claws deep into

John's carpet before she stalked off toward the bedroom.

Taking his gun from the holster he'd hung on a peg near the front door, John laid the weapon on the table and went back to his reading. It wasn't like him to be so jumpy, but then, it wasn't every day his father's disappearance came back to haunt him.

Or maybe it *had* haunted him every day. Maybe that was why he couldn't buy Gail Waters's suicide. Her connection to his father gave him a new reason to read this report again, to ask more questions, to finally have a chance to assuage the guilt that had eaten at him for seven long years, ever since Nick had accused him of being a traitor.

Even Tony hadn't been as hard on him as Nick had been. His youngest brother had been in love with Ashley Dallas at the time of her brutal murder. The two of them had attended a fraternity party at the university that night, and for some reason, Ashley had left the party early and alone. Just after midnight, her beaten and stabbed body had been found in a ditch near the frat house. The bloody murder weapon, a switchblade, had been found with Daniel O'Roarke's fingerprints on it.

Ashley's stepfather, Ed Dawson, then head of the Detective Division, insisted that Sean be put in charge of the investigation. He was, inarguably, the best detective in the department, and he and his team set about putting together a trail of evidence that would convict Daniel O'Roarke of Ashley's murder.

And then, weeks after the investigation began, Sean disappeared from his fishing cabin on Lake Michigan. Even though his body was never found, everyone assumed he'd been murdered by the O'Roarkes, maybe even by Daniel O'Roarke himself. The prosecutor was able to use the families' past history, along with forensic evidence from the murder weapon, to formulate a powerful case against Daniel. He'd been on death row for years now, awaiting appeal.

But John knew what none of the other detectives on his father's team had known, what his brothers still didn't know. Sean had confided to him and to Liam days before his disappearance that he was beginning to have doubts about Daniel O'Roarke's guilt.

Until this morning John and Liam had only spoken of that conversation one other time. The day Daniel O'Roarke's trial started, John had gone to his uncle, and the two of them had talked for a long time. Liam had told John how much pressure Sean had been under, from his job and from his failing marriage and, given the circumstances, it wasn't unusual for a detective to have doubts about his investigation.

"He should never have caught that case to begin with," Liam had told him. "Because of Tony's connection to the victim, Sean was bound to take a lot of heat. The pressure finally got to him. He started second-guessing himself, which is a dangerous thing for a detective."

"He'd been under pressure before," John had pointed out.

"Not like this." Liam's voice had hardened. "You go to that trial, Johnny, and you listen to the evidence. And then you come back here and tell me Daniel O'Roarke isn't guilty of murder."

John had done just that. He'd sat in the courtroom day in and day out and in the end, the evidence had proved persuasive, overwhelming really, even in the face of the O'Roarkes' high-powered attorneys.

In time John had come to accept Daniel O'Roarke's guilt, and he'd even managed to convince himself that his father was dead. He probably *had* been killed by the O'Roarkes. Sean Gallagher hadn't walked out on his family, leaving his eldest son to shoulder responsibilities that should never have been his. Besides, Nick would argue that John relished the job, anyway.

But now a reporter who had been investigating Sean's disappearance had died. Jumped off a five-story building, his uncle would have him believe. Even Roy seemed convinced of the suicide, or if not convinced, satisfied to have one less homicide on the books. Maybe it would be better for everyone involved if John rolled over on this one, too.

Think of the family, Liam had told him. Think of Tony and Nick and his mother. Even though she and John's father had had the kind of volatile relationship that almost always ended badly, Maggie Gallagher had been deeply affected by her husband's disappearance. In all these years she'd never remarried, never even once been on a date. It was almost as if she'd put her life on hold the day Sean disappeared, and she was waiting—maybe without realizing it—for him to come back home and finish their last argument.

So, okay. They'd all be better off if he just closed the Gail Waters case and pretended the suicide note stuffed in her pocket hadn't been too pat, the paper it was written on too clean—except for one smudged thumbprint that might or might not have been hers—and that she had a logical reason for being at that building on a Saturday night.

Maybe he could have swallowed all that and even more, if it wasn't for one thing—a tiny little girl with big brown eyes and a silent voice. A little girl who might be in big trouble if John closed his eyes and ears to a case that screamed bloody murder at him.

And what about Thea? She wouldn't welcome any more of his questions, he knew. She didn't want his help. But like it or not, he wasn't walking away. He couldn't. And the sooner she accepted that reality, the easier it would be on all of them.

BLISS KYLER OPENED the door almost immediately at Thea's knock. She looked a little startled, as if she'd been expecting someone else. "Mrs. Lockhart! What are you doing here? Is Nikki okay?"

"Nikki's fine. Could I talk to you for a moment?"

Bliss cast a nervous glance over her shoulder. "Sure. Come on in."

She was a beautiful girl, tall and willowy, with silvery-blond hair and cornflower-blue eyes fringed with long thick lashes that were, contrary to Mrs. Lewellyn's observation, quite real. With her exotic looks and knockout body, Bliss could easily have been a model or an actress, but instead, she wanted to be a teacher.

And she'd be a good one, too, Thea thought. Bliss was wonderful with Nikki, and Thea was very thankful for their chance meeting in the laundry room shortly after she and Nikki had moved into the building. Thea had found out that Bliss was a student at the university, struggling to make ends meet with her scholarship money and whatever odd jobs she could pick up that fit into her schedule.

Thea had asked her if she would be interested in helping with Nikki, and after supplying references, the two of them had struck a bargain. The arrangement had worked out well for both of them—until now. Now it appeared Bliss had gone directly against one of Thea's orders.

Bliss bent and scooped up a shirt and a pair of socks from the battered sofa, glancing at Thea apologetically. "I've been studying all night and haven't had a chance to pick up. And Eddie hasn't been feeling too well lately."

Eddie was her boyfriend, and although Bliss spoke of him fairly often, Thea had never met him. She tried not to let Mrs. Lewellyn's assessment of him influence her. The older woman's judgment could sometimes be harsh—though for whatever reason, she seemed taken with Thea and Nikki, if a little overprotective.

"I thought it was the flu at first," Bliss was saying with a weary sigh. "But now I'm not so sure."

She motioned toward the sofa, and the two of them perched on the edge.

"I'm sorry he's not feeling well," Thea murmured.

Bliss glanced toward the bedroom and lowered her voice. "He won't admit it, but I think he's upset by what happened here on Saturday night."

Thea said in surprise, "Are you talking about the woman who jumped off the roof?"

Bliss closed her eyes briefly, her lovely face suddenly drawn and sober. "Wasn't that horrible? That poor woman…" She shook her head sadly.

"Did Eddie know her?"

"That's the really strange part," Bliss said. "One of those odd coincidences that gives you goose bumps. Eddie and I saw her on television not too long ago. She was really gorgeous, but kind of cold, if you know what I mean, and Eddie made some comment about her being the type of woman who made older men do crazy things, like leave their wives and risk their careers. He said she looked as if she could…well, never mind. Eddie's not always the most tactful person. Anyway, we kidded around about her, but after we heard she was dead, it almost seemed as if we *did* know her. You know how it is when some actor dies, or some rock star you really like shoots himself.''

''You think that's why he's upset?'' Thea said doubtfully.

''Well, no. Not entirely.'' Bliss bit her lip worriedly. ''Eddie doesn't like to talk about his past, but he let it slip once that he had a stepsister who was murdered a few years ago. They were very close, and when she died, it took him a long time to get over it. I think somehow that woman's death Saturday night brought it all back to him. He's been in a really weird place ever since.''

A chill of unease slipped up Thea's backbone. Had Eddie known the dead woman? Was this something she should tell John?

But in the next instant she warned herself to stay out of it, to not get involved. Her main priority had to be protecting her daughter.

''I guess you know the police have been around asking questions,'' she said.

Bliss nodded. ''Eddie said someone came by here today, but I don't think he let him in. He wasn't in any mood to talk and, anyway, I don't know what Eddie could tell the police.''

''I think the detective probably wanted to see you,'' Thea told her.

Bliss's eyes widened. ''Me? Why?''

Thea hesitated. ''Did you take Nikki up to the roof on Saturday?''

A look of distress flashed through Bliss's eyes, followed closely by a glimmer of guilt. She chewed her lip. "I'm so sorry. I know I shouldn't have done it. Are you going to fire me?"

Thea ran a tired hand through her tangled curls. "Why did you do it? You know I don't want Nikki leaving the apartment without me, except to go to school."

"I know. But that's *why* I took her up there." Bliss's blue eyes reminded Thea of rain-soaked pansies. "You know how much I love Nikki, Mrs. Lockhart. I'd never do anything to hurt her. Saturday was just such a bad day. Both of us were a little down, and I thought we needed something to cheer us up. A change of pace. I knew you didn't want her leaving the building, so that's why I suggested a picnic on the roof."

"But it was freezing on Saturday."

"I know. But we bundled up, and it wasn't raining then. I just thought…" She drew a long breath and released it. "I thought Nikki needed to spread her wings a little."

"I see." Thea stared at Bliss. "You think I smother Nikki, don't you? You think I'm too protective."

"No. Oh, no," Bliss said earnestly. "I'd be exactly the same way in your place. I think you're a wonderful mother."

Sometimes Thea doubted that very much. How many other mothers killed their child's father? "I'm surprised she was willing to go up there with you. Nikki's afraid of heights. She won't even go down the slide at the playground."

"I know." Bliss's eyes glowed with excitement. "That's why I think that picnic may have been a major breakthrough for her."

A breakthrough that had come at the hands of a near

stranger, Thea thought, and tried not to feel resentful. What did it matter who was able to draw Nikki out of her self-imposed darkroom? Even if that person was John Gallagher?

And why did his name keep popping into her head? Why did his face keep haunting her daydreams?

She scrubbed her face with her hands, suddenly so weary she could hardly move. "Look, we'll talk about this later. What I really came down here to ask you was this. Did Nikki take her doll up to the roof when you had the picnic? Could she have left it up there?"

Bliss's face grew pensive as she considered the questions. "She did take her. I remember, because I fixed Piper a sandwich, too, just for fun. But we would never have left her there. I know how Nikki feels about that doll."

"Maybe Nikki put her down and forgot about her," Thea suggested.

Bliss shrugged. "It's possible. I remember it did get awfully cold up there, and I rolled everything up really fast when we got ready to leave. Maybe the doll fell out of the blanket." She paused, frowning, then said, "Is it lost?"

"Not anymore. Someone found it on the roof and returned it. I just wanted to know how she'd gotten up there in the first place."

Comprehension dawned in Bliss's blue eyes. "The police found her up there, didn't they? After that poor woman died. That's what they want to talk to me about, isn't it?"

Before Thea could answer, the bedroom door opened and a man wearing low-slung jeans and nothing else stood silhouetted in the murky light. His long dirty-blond hair framed a face that might once have been handsome, but now looked a bit dissipated. His goatee and the dark circles beneath his eyes only added to this impression. He had to be at least ten years older than Bliss.

"Eddie! I didn't hear you get up."

"Obviously." He folded his arms and leaned against the door frame. His voice was still groggy with sleep as his gaze checked out Thea. "You know what your problem is, Bliss? You don't seem to know how to keep your mouth shut."

"WE THE JURY FIND *the defendant guilty of murder in the first degree."*

"Guilty! Guilty! Guilty!" they all chanted, and then a police officer who looked like John but wasn't John led her into a small dark room where he strapped her to a table. A man in a white lab coat came at her with a huge needle.

"This won't hurt a bit," he said kindly.

"That's too good for a double murderess," the man who looked like John said coldly. "She should fry in the electric chair."

And then Rick's mother suddenly appeared at her side, her laugh sounding so much like her son's. "Nicolette's mine now. But don't you worry. I'll raise her just like I raised my Rick."

"No!" Thea screamed, and bolted upright in bed. The room was cold, but her skin was wet with perspiration. Shivering violently, she pulled the covers around her, huddling in bed as she glanced around the darkened room. What was she going to do?

Her first instinct was to grab Nikki and make a run for it, disappear into the night before John Gallagher could tie her to Gail Waters's death.

Once Thea had discovered how Nikki's doll had gotten on the roof, she'd hoped that would be the last of their involvement with the police. But now she knew that their involvement had only just begun.

If John was asking personal questions about their past, about their family and friends, then his suspicions were already aroused. It was only a matter of time before he uncovered the reason why Gail Waters had come to this building, and why Thea and Nikki had fled Baltimore. And when that happened, Thea's dream might become a terrifying reality.

Her heart started to pound. She could almost feel the noose tightening around her neck. If she was to die or go to prison, there would be no one to protect Nikki. Her little girl would be at the mercy of the Mancusos.

A wave of mind-numbing panic washed over her, but she fought to beat it back. She had to stay calm and rational for Nikki's sake. She would do anything to keep her daughter away from the ugliness that had colored Rick's life. Lenore Mancuso would never get her hands on Nikki.

Run! an inner voice still urged her. *Run and don't look back.*

But a quieter more logical voice reminded her there was risk in fleeing. To leave here now would mean exposing themselves once again—to chance detection by someone who might recognize them.

It would also arouse John's suspicions even more. Thea had seen the determination in his eyes, the tenacity in the way he pursued an investigation. She knew his type all too well. If she and Nikki ran, he would pursue them, hunt them relentlessly and ruthlessly. And there was every possibility he would lead the Mancusos straight to them.

But the most important reason not to run was Nikki. Dr. Nevin had stressed over and over to Thea the importance of a stable and loving environment. She'd told Thea last week they were nearing a critical stage in Nikki's therapy. To uproot her now, to destroy the fragile security Thea had built for them here might do irreparable damage.

So what was she supposed to do?

She could almost hear her father's advice. *Take matters into your own hands, sweet pea. Don't leave anything to fate.*

And it came to Thea almost in a flash exactly what had to be done. Although she'd concentrated almost exclusively on the business end of the firm, her father had enlisted her help from time to time in his investigations.

She remembered an instance in which one of his clients, a corporate wife, had been desperate to find out if her husband was conducting romantic trysts with his secretary in his office after hours.

Thea had posed as a member of the cleaning crew one night to gain entrance into the building. She'd not only gotten the proof her father and his client needed, but the adrenaline rush had been like nothing she'd ever experienced. Rick had told her once that cops had that same high chasing suspects through dark alleys or breaking down doors in the middle of the night.

Thea had been a lot younger then, and she hadn't had nearly as much at stake. She wasn't all that anxious to relive the excitement, but she could see no other way out of this mess. Tomorrow night she would go to Gail Waters's office. She would find and destroy any evidence that might link her, Thea, to Baltimore. And to the dead reporter.

She hoped and prayed she wasn't too late.

Chapter Six

Every Tuesday, after Thea picked up Nikki at her preschool, they rode the El to State Street in the Loop, where Dr. Nevin's office was located.

Even though Thea had lived all her life in a city, downtown Chicago was still daunting. The towering buildings rose like mountains toward the dismal gray sky, catching and trapping the wind from Lake Michigan in canyonlike streets, which were always clogged with traffic.

Thea could hardly imagine a colder bleaker landscape, and yet, there was an undercurrent of excitement in the hustle and bustle of the crowds, an almost breathtaking beauty in the diversity of the architecture, a timeless quality even in the wind that swirled snow flurries like bits of lace confetti.

Another time, under other circumstances, Thea would have adored Chicago. She would have enjoyed exploring the museums and galleries and the distinct neighborhoods that made the city so unique. She would have loved window-shopping along North Michigan Avenue, admiring the early Christmas displays, and then lunching on the waterfront, at the Navy Pier.

But for Thea and Nikki, Chicago had become little

more than a prison. Thea went to work and Nikki to school, and other than their visits to the park and to Dr. Nevin, they stayed inside as much as possible, minimizing the risk of detection.

Thea thought about their situation on the train ride back home that Tuesday. Dr. Nevin had reiterated how very important it was for Nikki to feel secure. "You have to be very, very careful, Thea. Any change in Nikki's routine, even one you and I might consider minor, could cause a severe setback."

Thea sighed, clasping Nikki's hand. She'd been so careful these past four months. That was what made getting caught up in a police investigation so ironic—and so scary. It made her all too aware of her limitations. There was only so much she could do to protect Nikki, but if anything, Thea was a fighter. She wouldn't give up without a battle.

Already she'd laid the groundwork for getting into Gail Waters's office that night. By making a few phone calls, she'd learned that the newspaper was on the bottom floor of an office building on LaSalle Street, and the janitorial services were subbed out to a company called Wendall's Pro Clean.

Then, just as she'd done years ago for her father, she'd called Wendall's, pretending to be someone from the newspaper who was dissatisfied with their services. During a conversation with a chatty secretary, Thea had learned not only the names of the two brothers who owned and operated the company—their marital status and private peccadilloes—but also the name of the foreman in charge of the crew scheduled to arrive at the paper at ten o'clock that evening.

Setting everything up had been almost too easy, but she had always been good at extracting information from people. Her father had told her once she'd missed her calling. She should have been an investigator, or even an actress, but she'd quickly reminded him that her skills weren't exactly lost in the world of business.

She tried to use those memories to buoy her confidence, but in spite of all her planning, she knew that something could go very wrong tonight. If she was caught breaking into Gail Waters's office, she would not only likely be charged with the reporter's murder, but she would also be sent back to Baltimore to stand trial for Rick's.

And Nikki would be sent to live with Lenore Mancuso.

As she and Nikki got off the train at the Cottage Grove station, Thea shivered with the cold. Maybe she was wrong about all this. Maybe Gail Waters being at the apartment building the night she died had been nothing more than a coincidence. Maybe there was nothing incriminating in her files.

But that wasn't a chance Thea could afford to take.

RATHER THAN WALKING the several blocks back to their apartment, as she would have done if she'd been alone, Thea hailed a cab. She had the driver let them off at a nearby market, and she and Nikki went inside to pick out something for dinner. By the time they came back out, it was growing dark and the snow was coming down in earnest. They trudged homeward, but as they neared the stoop of their building, Thea paused under a streetlight.

The snow was so beautiful that for a moment she forgot the cold and the wind and what she might have to do that night to protect her daughter. Her fingers tightened around Nikki's gloved hand as the two of them stood on the sidewalk, caught up in a swirling fairyland of white.

For some reason there wasn't much traffic on the street, and the city noises seemed muted by the snow. It was like being in a water globe, cocooned from the outside world. The silence—such glorious silence—had a spiritual quality to it, a healing peacefulness that seemed to touch the deepest part of Thea's soul. As she lifted her face to the cold softness, a profound awareness came over her.

Kneeling, she set the grocery bag on the wet street and placed her hands on her daughter's shoulders. Gazing into Nikki's eyes, she whispered, "I think I understand now."

Nikki gazed back at her, solemn and sweet, and Thea whispered fiercely, "I love you so much."

Still silent, Nikki captured a snowflake on her fingertip and touched it to Thea's lips. Thea smiled, comprehending, and then, to her surprise and joy, Nikki stuck out her tongue, like any other child, and tasted the snow.

Thea's smile turned into a laugh, and she rose, lifting Nikki into her arms and whirling her round and round. For an instant their troubles faded, and they were caught up in a moment of pure happiness. Something significant had happened to both of them in that quiet moment. Thea wasn't sure she could explain it, even to Dr. Nevin, but she knew just the same that her daughter was going to be all right. They both were.

She set Nikki down and bent to pick up the damp grocery sack. "Let's go have dinner."

They walked up the steps, and Thea, balancing the grocery sack in one arm, unlocked the door. Once inside, the warmth enveloped them, and as they climbed the stairs to the second floor, Thea felt more hopeful than she had in months, maybe even years.

Perhaps that was why seeing Morris Dalrimple at her door—as if he had just stepped from her apartment—provoked such a strong reaction in her.

"What do you think you're doing?" she called harshly.

He jumped as if a canon had gone off near his ear. His eyes widened when he saw Thea and Nikki standing at the top of the stairs.

Thea had to fight the urge to grab Nikki and back away. She couldn't help remembering what Mrs. Lewellyn had said to her.

Ax murderers sometimes claim they have good intentions, but their victims are still just as dead....

In spite of her trepidation, she moved down the hall to her door. Having gathered his wits about him again, Morris Dalrimple smiled and held out a piece of white paper. "For you."

Thea reluctantly accepted his offering. "What is it?"

"An, er, invitation. Mama and I would like for you and little Nikki to come down some afternoon for, er, tea."

"Well, I—"

"Would tomorrow be convenient?"

He looked so expectant Thea had a hard time dashing his hopes—ax murderer or not.

"This is very kind of you and your mother, but I rarely socialize, Mr. Dalrimple."

"Call me Dal, please. All my friends do. Won't you reconsider?" he all but pleaded. "It would mean so much to Mama. She doesn't get out much, you know, but she's, er, seen you and your little girl coming and going from her bedroom window. She's quite taken with both of you. Please say you'll come…Thea. May I call you Thea?''

No way she would subject Nikki to even a couple of hours with Morris Dalrimple. He and his mother might be perfectly lovely people once you got to know them, but just standing here in the hallway, Thea felt uneasy. There was something very disturbing about the way he looked at her, something almost sinister, as Mrs. Lewellyn had suggested.

''I'll have to let you know,'' Thea said evasively. ''Right now I need to get Nikki inside. She hasn't had her dinner yet.'' She glanced pointedly, at the grocery bag in her arms.

Mr. Dalrimple nodded. ''Of course. I understand. But I really do hope you'll come. There's something I, er, need to discuss with you.''

Oh, no, Thea thought in dread. She unlocked her door, hoping to escape inside. She could hear his raspy breathing behind her, and a shiver crawled up her backbone.

''It's about that woman who died. That, er, reporter.''

Another shiver. Thea turned to him slowly. ''What about her?''

''Didn't you recognize her?''

Thea's stomach twisted in warning. ''What do you mean?''

He lowered his voice conspiratorially. ''I don't think we should, er, speak about it in front of the child.''

Thea opened the door and reached inside to switch on the light. Her gaze automatically swept the room, making sure nothing was out of place. She said to Nikki, ''Why don't you go on inside, sweetie? You can turn on the TV, or color for a few minutes while I talk to Mr. Dalrimple. I'll leave the door open so I can see you.''

Nikki, ever obedient, did as she was told. Thea waited until her daughter had gathered up her coloring book and crayons from the dining table and brought them over to the floor in front of the television, where Thea could see her. Nikki chose a crayon, red as always, and began stroking up and down the page, seemingly unmindful of the picture.

Thea turned back to Mr. Dalrimple. "What do you mean, didn't I recognize her?" she asked again.

He looked as if he'd said more than he meant to. "Perhaps I shouldn't have mentioned that. I'm, er, helping the police with their investigation. I must be discreet."

"I'm sure they're very lucky to have your help," Thea said, automatically reverting back to her old instincts. Flattery could sometimes get you everywhere.

Mr. Dalrimple preened with pleasure. "Well, yes. I'm not without some, er, experience in these matters."

"I didn't realize."

Again he looked as if he regretted his words. "All I meant was, Mama and I love watching cop shows on television. We never miss an episode of 'America's Most Wanted.' It's a very informative program."

"I'm sure it is," Thea murmured. She paused. "Getting back to Gail Waters. Did you recognize her that night…Dal?"

He turned coy. "Did you?"

"I never saw her before in my life. But you intimated just a moment ago that you *did* recognize her."

He cocked his head, regarding her curiously. "You know, I never noticed before, but the way you speak,

the words you use…you seem very educated for a waitress.''

Thea's heart catapulted into her throat, but she
forced her voice to remain even. ''Waitresses go to
school, too, you know, and besides, like you, I watch
a lot of television.''

''That explains it,'' he said, but Thea realized he
wasn't at all fooled by her explanation. He was a lot
cleverer than she and Mrs. Lewellyn had given him
credit for, and maybe a lot more sinister. As if reading
her thoughts, he said softly, ''I'm in a unique position
to help you, Thea.''

She suddenly felt as if she needed to go inside and
wash her hands. ''What do you mean?''

''The police trust me. They buy everything I tell
them.''

''What *did* you tell them?''

''The truth. I didn't recognize Gail Waters that night.
I still have no idea how she got inside this building. It
wasn't until I saw her, er, picture the next day on TV
that I remembered seeing her before.''

''Where?''

''She came here a few weeks ago looking for you.''

''Me?'' Thea could feel the grocery bag slipping
from her suddenly wooden arms, and with an effort,
she heaved it upward.

''She didn't know your name, of course, but I knew
from her description she was talking about you and
Nikki. She said she'd come to, er, visit a friend in the
building one day and saw you and Nikki outside. She
thought she recognized you as someone she went to
school with. She wanted to know your name and which
apartment you lived in.''

And then it hit Thea why Gail Waters had looked

vaguely familiar to her. The image came back to her in a bright damning flash.

Thea and Nikki were coming home one day just as an attractive blonde was leaving. They met on the steps outside and exchanged brief glances and polite smiles.

"What a beautiful little girl," the woman had remarked in passing.

Thea, accustomed to strangers admiring her daughter's beauty, had murmured, "Thank you," and then promptly forgotten the episode as she and Nikki went into their apartment to hole up for the coming night.

That woman had been Gail Waters. She must have recognized them. That was why she'd come back to ask questions, but…if she hadn't known about them until then, who had she come here to see that day? Who was this "friend" she'd been visiting? The same person who had let her in the night she died?

"She obviously mistook me for someone else," Thea said with a shrug.

"Obviously," he agreed. "But if the police found out she was asking questions about you, they could, er, make life, er, uncomfortable for you, if you know what I mean."

"I see your point," Thea murmured. "What do you suggest I do about it?"

He smiled slyly. "I have some ideas. If you come down for tea tomorrow afternoon, perhaps even dinner tomorrow night, you, Mama and I could figure out what to do."

As a bribe Thea had seen more subtle ones. "What about Nikki?"

"Perhaps it might be best if you left her with Mrs. Lewellyn. We wouldn't want to, er, distress her any further, would we?"

Watch out for that man, Thea, dear. I don't care at all for the way he looks at you.... He's always very quick to speak so lovingly of his mother, but how long has it been since you've seen her?

He'd eliminated Nikki from the equation, and somehow Thea doubted Mrs. Dalrimple would be making an appearance tomorrow night, either. Thea wasn't quite sure yet how she planned to deal with him, but she knew one thing for certain. She wouldn't be having tea in that creepy little man's apartment tomorrow night or any other night.

"I'll have to talk to Mrs. Lewellyn," she said. Before he could offer any more persuasions, footsteps sounded on the stairs. John Gallagher appeared at the top, silhouetted for a moment in the dim hallway light. He came toward them, and Thea was absurdly glad to see him.

Beside her, Mr. Dalrimple pulled himself up to his full height of five-two or five-three. He drew a long rasping breath as if he was very nervous. "I see you're making use of the, er, key I provided you, Detective."

"It's come in very handy." John's gaze flashed from Dalrimple to Thea. His eyes narrowed, as if he was wondering what might be going on between them.

Nothing, Thea wanted to assure him. But that wasn't exactly true. Thanks to Dalrimple's revelation about Gail Waters, he and Thea had suddenly become co-conspirators against the police. It was a position she found very uncomfortable. She didn't like being indebted to Morris Dalrimple. She didn't like him period, and even worse, she didn't trust him. He was up to something, and her suspicions left a distinctly bad taste in her mouth.

The damp shopping bag picked that precise moment

to collapse, and in spite of her hand beneath the bottom, two apples tumbled from the split paper and thudded onto the carpet. John retrieved them, then placing his own huge hand beneath the bag, took it from her. "Looks as if you could use a little help."

He was good, Thea thought grudgingly, because now she had no choice but to invite him in.

The same notion must have occurred to Mr. Dalrimple, because he muttered, "I should have thought of that myself."

John said, "Where do you want this?"

"In the kitchen." She started to follow him inside, but Mr. Dalrimple caught her arm. It was all Thea could do not to brush his hand away as she would an annoying fly.

"I would, er, caution you to watch what you say around him," he said in a low voice.

"Thanks for the warning." She tried to turn away, but his grasp only tightened.

"I'll do everything I can to protect you and your little girl. You can count on me."

Thea wanted to tell him she didn't want or need his protection, but until she learned what was in Gail Waters's files, and what, if anything, Dalrimple had found out, she wasn't in any position to antagonize him.

If she'd had any residual doubts about what she planned to do tonight, Dalrimple's insinuation—what later might turn out to be extortion—had cleared the last of them away.

SHE SEEMED EVEN EDGIER than usual, John thought as he watched Thea move about the tiny kitchen, putting away her groceries. Nikki was coloring at the coffee table, and except for a brief curious glance when he'd spoken to her, she was busy pretending he didn't exist.

He was surprised by how much he'd looked forward to seeing the little girl again, and how much he wanted to get a reaction from her. He'd never been around kids that much, never even thought he wanted to be. There might have been a time when he'd had some vague notion of starting a family with Meredith, but they had never really talked about it. Which, considering what had happened between them, was a good thing.

John couldn't explain why he was so drawn to Nikki, or to her mother, for that matter. He just was. Probably more than was wise.

He watched Nikki color for a moment, then turned back to Thea. The simple lines of her pink uniform did nothing to conceal her slim waist nor the tantalizing curve of her breasts and hips. She was a small woman, but she had a powerful presence, an impact that was undeniable.

Something tightened inside him, and he realized how much he wanted to touch her. There was a sexual element naturally—what man wouldn't want her? But what he really craved at that moment was, surprisingly, tenderness. The feel of her hair beneath his lips. The touch of her fingertips against his face. The whispered acknowledgment of feelings that ran a lot deeper than the bedroom.

He thought of the good times with Meredith, the quiet dinners, the summer strolls along the lake, the winter evenings before a fire. Those were the things he missed about being married. The sex had been a bonus.

As if sensing his gaze on her, Thea turned. A hint of color washed across her cheeks, but she lifted her chin, as if to deny her reaction. "Thank you for helping me with the groceries."

"No problem."

"I…don't want to keep you."

He gave her an ironic smile. "That was subtle."

"I'm sorry." Her blush deepened. "I didn't mean to be rude."

She was one of the most interesting women John had ever met. Transparent one moment and completely guarded the next. She would keep a man on his toes, he had no doubt. "Luckily I've got a tough skin. Couldn't be a cop without it."

"That's true, I guess." And then, without warning, she returned his smile.

John had thought her attractive before, but she was absolutely beautiful when she smiled. Her dark hair seemed glossier, her brown eyes deeper, her lips…

Those lips were made for kissing. For devouring. Suddenly tenderness was the last thing he desired from Thea. He wanted her to walk around that bar and rip off his shirt, press her body against his and—

John gave a start when he felt a tiny hand slip into his. Glancing down, he saw Nikki at his side, not looking at him, not saying anything, just standing there holding his hand. And the bottom of his world dropped right out from under him.

He glanced at Thea. She was staring at her daughter, her expression stunned, her face so pale he thought for a moment she might pass out. Then slowly she lifted her gaze to meet his. There was confusion and wonder in her eyes, and a glimmer of something that might have been fear.

"I've never seen her do that," she whispered. "Even

before…'' She put trembling fingertips to her lips, clearly overcome with emotion.

John wasn't sure what he was supposed to do or say. How he was supposed to react. He knew he couldn't stand here forever holding the kid's hand, and yet…he was reluctant to break the contact. Reluctant to diminish the warm glow that seemed to radiate from somewhere deep inside him. He felt as if he'd shared in a miracle in some small way, and the experience was humbling.

He cleared his throat, but before he could figure out what to say, Thea came to his rescue. ''I think she's asking you to dinner.''

As invitations went, it was a fairly devastating one.

''DINNER WAS GREAT,'' John said, lifting his coffee cup to his lips. Nikki had gotten so sleepy halfway through the meal that Thea had already tucked her and Piper into bed. She and John were alone over the remnants of salad and spaghetti, and she had to refrain from glancing at the clock. The minutes were ticking away. If she was going to Gail Waters's office tonight…

''It was nothing special,'' she said. ''The sauce came from a jar.'' And then she felt herself blush again. She had no idea why John's presence had such a powerful effect on her. She wasn't some lovestruck schoolgirl. After her experience with Rick, she'd promised herself never to be vulnerable again, and yet there was still a part of her that wanted to believe in love.

She didn't remember her mother, but her father and Mona had had a very special relationship, a closeness that, rather than excluding Thea, had drawn her into the warmth of their love.

That was the way it should be, she thought with an inward sigh. That was what she wanted someday for herself and Nikki. Only…not with a cop. Never with a cop.

John Gallagher was nothing like Rick, but her situation made it impossible for Thea to become involved with anyone, let alone a police detective. John already had suspicions about her. He'd already been asking questions. She was crazy to even be spending this time with him. She'd invited him to dinner only because Nikki had responded so strongly to his presence. Thea had taken that as a positive sign. A wonderful sign. But now it was time for him to go.

She rose and started clearing the table. He followed her, but she quickly said, "Don't bother. It'll just take me a minute to clean up. And I'm sure you have more important things to do."

"Again, not too subtle."

Thea shrugged. "I'm sorry. But it's getting late, and I have to be at work early in the morning."

"You turn in at—" he glanced at his watch "—seven-forty-three?"

"Sometimes. When I've been on my feet all day." She saw him glance at her legs, and then slowly and deliberately his gazed moved over her.

She was acutely aware of how she must look to him. She hadn't bothered changing out of her uniform, and she knew her hair must be a mess. Whatever makeup she'd slung on that morning before dashing off to work had long since faded. Thea realized it had been some time since she'd felt attractive, and since she'd cared.

But now was not the time to get vain. She ran her fingers through her tangled curls. "You must have an early day, too."

"I have the first watch, but it usually spills over into the second. Sometimes the third."

"Is that why you came here tonight?" she couldn't resist asking. "Are you on official business?"

"As a matter of fact, yes. I came here to talk to your baby-sitter, Bliss Kyler. I haven't been able to track her down yet."

Thea just looked at him. "So you still don't believe me about Nikki's doll."

"I didn't say that." He reached for his coat on the hook by the front door. "I wouldn't be much of a detective if I didn't follow up on every lead, now would I?"

She watched him shrug into his coat. The collar was turned up, framing his handsome face. His eyes were very blue tonight, and intense, but not cold as she'd once thought them.

"Bliss will tell you exactly what I told you," she said.

"Then you shouldn't mind if I talk to her."

"I don't mind."

"Good."

"It's just…" Thea paused, wondering how far she dared go. She wrapped her arms around her middle and stared up at him. "I can't help wondering what it will take to convince you that Nikki and I don't have anything to do with this."

"You still don't get it, do you?" He was standing at the door, a tall imposing man who had too much power over her—in more ways than one. His gaze was still intense, but the warmth was gone, replaced by a steely determination that made Thea shiver. The attraction was still there, too, but he wouldn't let it get in his way, she knew. He was too much of a professional for that.

"Get what?" Thea demanded.

"This isn't about you. This is about a possible homicide, and someone who may already have killed once in cold blood. Do you think a murderer would hesitate to kill again if he thought there was a witness to his crime?"

Cold fear knotted in her stomach. "But Nikki didn't see anything. She wasn't on that roof Saturday night."

"Then let's make sure everyone else knows it, too."

His statement hit Thea with the subtlety of a bomb. He wasn't trying to prove Nikki was a witness. He was trying to prove she wasn't. He was trying to make sure if Gail Waters *was* murdered, the killer wouldn't come after Nikki.

Thea started to tremble all over. "I still want to believe she committed suicide."

John shrugged. "Maybe she did. But I'm not willing to turn my head and take that chance. Not where Nikki is concerned."

Thea felt tears sting behind her lids. She and Nikki had been on their own for so long. The temptation to let someone else take care of them was almost overpowering, but it wouldn't work. It couldn't work. Not with a police detective.

She bit her lip. "I guess I should thank you for...caring."

"Hard to believe, isn't it?"

"What?"

He touched his fist to her chin. "That a cop has feelings. We're not all macho men with John Wayne complexes."

"I never said you were." But of course, there'd been a time when she'd thought exactly that.

"Most of us are just ordinary guys with mortgages and families and the same problems as everyone else."

You're wrong, Thea thought. *There's nothing ordinary about you.*

He was no ordinary cop, either. Which was why he scared her so much.

"You'd better go," she said. *Before I do something stupid.*

But the choice was suddenly taken out of her hands. He bent swiftly and touched his mouth to hers. Thea parted her lips automatically and her eyes drifted closed, yielding to the kiss—wanting it—before she realized what she was doing. She was kissing a man who had the power to destroy her and her little girl.

Before she could move away from him, John straightened, threading his fingers through her hair for one brief moment as he gazed down into her upturned face. "Good night, Thea."

She stared, stunned, at the door he closed between them.

Chapter Seven

A short while later John was northbound on Michigan Avenue when his cell phone rang. His thoughts were still on Thea as he answered the call. Her lips had been so incredibly soft—

"I need to see you, Johnny." His uncle's voice cut across the air waves. "This can't wait until morning."

John switched on his wiper blades. The snow had started coming down again once he'd left Thea's building, and the streets were getting treacherous. "You still at the station?"

"No, I'm at the house. Swing by here before you go home."

"What's this about, Liam?"

"We'll talk when you get here."

Twenty minutes later John was driving through the old south-side neighborhood where he and his brothers and cousins had all grown up, and where his mother still lived with his grandmother, Colleen. His grandfather had died a few years ago, and St. Anne's had been packed with officers in full dress uniform, from beat cops all the way up to the superintendent, who had come to pay their last respects to William Gallagher.

There had been no such tribute for John's father, whose case was still technically active. Every once in a while a detective in the cold-case squad would take out the file and reexamine the evidence, but nothing new had turned up—until now.

The porch light was on at his uncle's house. John parked in the driveway, and Liam opened the door almost immediately, as if he'd been standing at the window watching for John. John shook the snow from his coat and stamped his shoes before following his uncle inside.

A fire crackled in the fireplace in the den, and a half-empty whiskey glass sat on an oak coffee table. The *Sun-Times* lay scattered about the floor and sofa, and John wondered if his aunt was out of town. Helen Gallagher was something of a neat freak, the polar opposite of Liam, but somehow the two had managed to coexist peacefully for almost forty years. As Gallagher marriages went, theirs was one of the more successful.

"Sit down, Johnny. Care for a drink?" Liam picked up his own glass and swirled the amber liquid, then lowered his frame into a recliner near the fireplace.

John shook his head. "No, thanks. What did you want to see me about?"

Liam took a long swallow of whiskey. "I got a call from the superintendent today. It seems the Gail Waters case has caught his attention."

"Why? Was I right in thinking she might have contacted him before she died?"

Liam leaned forward, lowering his voice even though John suspected they were alone in the house. His uncle's eyes were bloodshot, making John wonder how long he'd been hitting the bottle. "What I'm about to tell you can't leave this room."

Uneasy, John managed a casual shrug. "Whatever you say."

Liam sat back in his chair. "The superintendent thinks his son may be living in the building where Gail Waters died."

"You mean Eddie?" John stared at his uncle in shock. He hadn't seen or heard anything of Eddie Dawson in years. Once, they'd all lived in this same neighborhood, been taught by the same nuns at St. Anne's, played in the same park, but that was before Eddie's stepsister was murdered, before Ed Dawson began rising in the department ranks. Months after Ashley's death, Dawson had moved the family into a swanky condo on Lake Shore Drive.

Just as John and his brothers had done, Eddie had followed his father and grandfather onto the force. But he hadn't been able to cut it, and he'd left the department under a cloud of controversy, much to his father's embarrassment. But Dawson had managed to quiet the speculation surrounding Eddie's departure from the force, just as he'd kept Eddie's name out of the official report on Ashley's death.

"His name wasn't on the tenant list," John told his uncle.

"Dawson thinks he's living there with some girl."

"What girl?"

"He didn't say. I'm not sure he even knows. He's worried that Gail Waters may have gone there that night to talk to Eddie about Ashley's murder. He might have been the one who let her in."

John exploded. "Why the hell didn't he tell us this before?"

"He just found out."

"What do you mean, he just found out? He didn't know where Eddie was living?"

Liam shrugged. "Dawson hasn't heard from Eddie in years, not since the kid left the force. Annette's the one who kept in touch with him. I guess she went to Dawson after she read about the case in the paper." His uncle paused. "You heard they split up?"

John had heard all right. There was a lot of talk around the department that the superintendent was involved with a younger woman, but John hoped those rumors weren't true. He'd always felt a little sorry for Annette Dawson. He didn't think she'd ever gotten over Ashley's death.

"Evidently Annette is worried that Eddie might get dragged into the investigation somehow."

John said bluntly, "Is she also worried Eddie might have had something to do with Gail Waters's death?"

"For your sake, I hope you don't repeat that." Liam's voice was traced with something that might have been a warning.

"Why?" John demanded. "If Eddie's innocent, what are they so worried about?"

"Having the media rehash Ashley's murder. You can understand that, can't you, Johnny? I don't want to see Sean's name dragged through the papers again, either. But if some reporter connects Eddie to Gail Waters, it wouldn't take much digging to find out she was investigating Sean's disappearance when she died. The rest is bound to come out, too."

"Maybe it needs to come out," John said slowly. "Let's think about this for a minute. Eddie Dawson was at that party seven years ago when Ashley was murdered. Tony and Miles both swore they saw him, but somehow his name never made it into the official report. Now you're telling me he may be somehow connected to Gail Waters's death. I don't think this is something we can sweep under the rug, Liam.''

His uncle shrugged, but he didn't seem quite able to meet John's gaze. ''I talked to Miles. He's not so sure anymore Eddie was there that night. He thinks he and Tony may have been mistaken.''

John glared at him, a suspicion of something ugly slithering inside him. His cousin, Miles, had always been an ambitious man. ''What dimmed Miles's memory? The prospect of a promotion?''

''I'm going to forget you said that,'' Liam said coldly. He sat forward again and placed his empty glass on the coffee table. ''I'm thinking about the family, Johnny, and you should, too. If someone starts digging into Ashley's murder, looking for a scandal, Eddie Dawson's name isn't the only one that could turn up.''

''Meaning?''

''I think you know what I mean.'' Liam heaved himself out of his chair and went to replenish his drink. Instead of taking the recliner when he returned, he stood with his back to the fireplace, as if suddenly chilled. ''What do you think would happen if some hot-to-trot reporter got a notion to make a martyr out of Daniel O'Roarke? Hell, it's already happened. O'Roarke's got his own web site, from what I hear, and a bunch of death-row groupies who think he's some kind of hero. If that same reporter started looking for other suspects in Ashley's murder, who do you think is going to come off looking guiltier? Her stepbrother or her jilted lover?''

A thrill of alarm shot up John's backbone. ''What the hell are you talking about?''

''I'm talking about your brother, Tony. He and Ashley had a heated argument at that party. That's why she left without him. Tony had too much to drink and passed out after she left. He didn't even remember the fight, but Miles came and told me about it the next day. He told Sean, too.''

"If that's true, why wasn't it in the report?'' John rose and faced his uncle. He didn't much like what Liam was implying.

"Because Sean left it out. He wanted to protect Tony just as Dawson wanted to protect Eddie. And under the same circumstances, I would have done the same for Miles. We look out for our own, Johnny. That's how it works.''

"Including suppressing evidence?'' John turned away from Liam in disgust. "I don't believe this. I don't believe *any* of this. And I sure as hell don't believe what you're asking me to do.''

"It's the only way,'' his uncle said quietly. "If Gail Waters committed suicide, all this other stuff goes away.''

John glared at him. "And if she was murdered?''

"There's no proof she was.''

"Maybe not yet. But we're still going through her files, tracking down leads. This case is far from over.''

Liam just shook his head. "I would think about this long and hard if I were you. If Daniel O'Roarke's attorneys get even a hint of what you and I have talked about tonight, they'll file an appeal so fast our heads will spin. Hell, they might even get his trial overturned. And then that bastard walks. Can you live with that, Johnny? Can you live with being a party to setting your own father's murderer free?''

"I don't know that I can live with what you're asking me to do, either,'' John said, suddenly bone-deep weary.

''If Daniel O'Roarke is exonerated because of this, then Ashley's case will have to be reopened. Your own brother could become a suspect. Considering his record, Tony would probably be suspended, and that might be enough to finally push him over the edge.'' Liam paused, his eyes now clear and coldly alert. ''And this time, Sean won't be around to protect him.''

As soon as John's car left the driveway, the kitchen door opened, and Superintendent Ed Dawson walked into Liam's den. He was a tall man, big but not overweight. As always, he'd forgone his uniform for an expensive gray suit and custom-made blue shirt, and his thick silver hair hadn't been cut by any barber. Liam could smell cologne all the way across the room, and he wrinkled his nose in distaste. Ed Dawson had turned into a real—

''Do you think you convinced him?'' Dawson demanded, helping himself to Liam's whiskey. He knew where the glasses and the liquor were kept. In the old days he and Sean would come over on Sunday afternoons, and the three of them would sit around getting drunk while they watched the Bears beat the hell out of the Packers. Neither Annette Dawson nor Sean's wife, Maggie, would put up with their shenanigans, but Helen had never minded. She was a good wife, Liam thought. Better than he deserved.

''Johnny's a good cop,'' he said. ''And he's family. Once he gives it some thought, he won't go against us on this.''

''He's not a rogue like his brother, you mean.''

''Tony's okay,'' Liam said, automatically defending

the boy. He didn't always condone his behavior, but he was still family.

"What about the witness John mentioned yesterday? Anything pan out there?"

Liam frowned. The little girl could be a problem. So far, it looked as if that was a dead end, but if it turned out otherwise...

"There's nothing to it," he told Dawson. "False lead."

Dawson walked toward the fireplace, sipping his whiskey. His gaze met Liam's in the firelight. "I've been watching John for some time now. I'm impressed with what I see. I'd like to see him move up."

For just an instant, jealousy stabbed through Liam, cold and hard like a knife blade. Not for himself, but for Miles. His son was a damn fine cop, too, but a narc didn't get the spotlight like the homicide detectives. Maybe because they spent so much of their time undercover.

Still, it was good to know that *one* of the Gallaghers had caught himself an angel. There'd been a time when Liam had thought he might someday be appointed superintendent, but he hadn't had the right connections. Now it looked as if Sean's oldest boy might be the first Gallagher to make Chicago's top cop. And maybe that was fitting somehow.

"I'm counting on you to keep this thing under control," Dawson said, and Liam didn't miss the warning in his voice. Liam was set to retire in another few years. He didn't need this kind of trouble.

"It's under control," he said, but a sliver of fear wedged somewhere deep inside his chest. Johnny was a good cop, no mistake about that. But he could be stubborn as hell if he thought he was in the right.

Sean had been like that, too. He hadn't known when to give up or when to look the other way.

And see where it had gotten him?

THEA SAT IN THE BACK of a cab and stared across the street at the building that housed the *Press,* a small paper with an almost infinitesimal circulation, from all she'd been able to learn. Gail Waters had been the driving force behind the newspaper's meager success, as well as the cable show, *Vanished!,* which had been her brainchild.

There was no guarantee, of course, that the police hadn't already found incriminating information in her office, but the fact that Thea was still free was a good sign. Maybe the cops hadn't known what they were looking for.

The heater was running in the cab, and the back windows had started to fog up. Using her glove, Thea cleared herself a porthole. She glanced at her watch. It wasn't quite ten. She still had a few minutes before the cleaning crew showed up.

She used the time to go over her plan again. After John had left her apartment, she'd called Mrs. Lewellyn to come and stay with Nikki, and then she'd called a cab to take her to LaSalle Street, across the river, where the paper's office was located. Using a taxi, instead of the El, was yet another extravagance, but Thea had been worried about running late. And she hadn't wanted to stand out on the street for an extended period of time.

This will work, she told herself firmly. She'd done it before, and she could do it again.

But her heart started pumping desperately when she saw a white panel van pull into the alley beside the building. Wendall's Pro Clean was emblazoned on the side, and almost immediately four women and one man piled from the vehicle. The man opened the back doors, and they all began to arm themselves with cleaning supplies and mop buckets. The heavier equipment— vacuum cleaners and floor buffers—were either stored inside the building or left in the van to be fetched later.

Paying the cabdriver, Thea climbed out and hurried across the street. The man, who wore dark blue coveralls with the name of the cleaning service stitched across his left breast pocket, was a wiry little guy probably somewhere in his late fifties. He gave a start when Thea came up to him.

"Jesus, girl, where the hell did *you* come from?"

"Are you Mr. Tully?"

He gave her a suspicious glare. "Who wants to know?"

"Mr. Wendall told me I should come here and talk to you tonight."

"Mr. Wendall?" He scowled. "Tom or Barry?"

She paused only fractionally. "Barry."

"That figures." Tully gave her the once-over. "You look to be his type." He said over his shoulder to one of the women, "Young and breathing."

The woman laughed appreciatively and shook her dark head. "That Barry's a card all right."

Tully turned back to Thea. "So what do you want?"

She lowered her eyes, as if overcome by self-doubt. "H-he said you could put me to work tonight, and if I did okay, he would give me a full-time job."

"He did, did he? Well, I got news for you. I ain't running no baby-sitting service here."

Thea lifted her gaze in supplication. "Please. I really need this job, Mr. Tully. My little girl's sick and my husband's done took off..." She let her desperation linger in the way she bit her trembling lip.

Thea thought she heard the woman behind Tully mutter disgustedly, "Men. Damn no-count loafers."

Tully handed the woman a key. "Go on now, the lot of you. We ain't paying you to stand around out here gawking. I'll take care of this."

The women did as they were told, the one with the key unlocking the side door and then glancing back at Thea curiously once she and the others were inside.

Tully's eyes narrowed on Thea. "This ain't the normal way we do things. Why didn't you come to the shop and clock in, same as the rest of us?"

"I live near here," Thea explained, letting her teeth chatter in the cold. It added to the effect, and it wasn't difficult to do. She was cold and nervous. "And I didn't need to clock in because I agreed to work tonight for nothing."

"For nothing, huh? Nothing's for nothing." Tully gave her a sidelong glance as he closed the van doors. "You'd best remember that, girl. Especially where Barry Wendall is concerned."

"Please, Mr. Tully, give me a chance. You can call Barry—I mean, Mr. Wendall if you feel you need to."

Tully gave a short laugh. "And where would you suggest I call him? D.J.'s Dollhouse? It's cheerleader night or some damn thing."

Thea had never heard of the place, but she suspected it was a strip joint. Evidently Mr. Tully didn't think too highly of his employer, or at least one of them. "Should I just go back home then?" Thea let her shoulders slump beneath her coat. "I can call Mr. Wendall tomorrow."

Tully let out a long sigh, as if he was put upon all

too frequently. His breath frosted in the cold air as he gave her a long sharp appraisal. "You don't look like you weigh a hundred pounds soaking wet. Are you sure you can handle this kind of work?"

"Try me." A little more confidence and less desperation this time. Thea knew she had him.

"You have to provide your own uniform," he warned. "We're all required to wear 'em. Company policy."

"Yes, I know. Mr. Wendall told me that, so I borrowed one." Thea unbuttoned her coat, letting him glimpse her waitress uniform beneath. "If I'm hired on permanent, I'll get the kind I'm supposed to have." She paused again. "I'm a very hard worker, Mr. Tully. If you give me this chance, you won't be sorry."

He cocked his head. "You right sure it was Barry who sent you?"

Thea shrugged. "How would I know about him if he hadn't?"

Tully didn't seem to have an answer for that. "Okay," he said. "I guess we'll give you a shot. But every newbie has to start with the toilets. That's *my* policy. You got a problem with it?"

"No, I don't," Thea said convincingly. She'd do a lot worse than scrub toilets for a chance to look in Gail Waters's files.

TULLY MADE IT his personal business to see that Thea got properly initiated. They started on the fifth floor of the building and for almost an hour, he stood over her shoulder, supervising her work. He didn't let her out of his sight.

"Not exactly glamorous work, is it?" He looked almost sympathetic. "I'm gonna step outside and have a smoke. You be okay while I'm gone?"

"Sure." Thea straightened and massaged her lower back.

"There's a vending area near the stairwell on the first floor. You can take yourself a break in another hour or so."

"Thanks. I'll be ready for something to drink." She went back to her work, but the minute she heard the washroom door close, she got to her feet and hurried to the door.

Glancing out into the hallway, she saw the elevator doors closing and then the car descended. She took the stairs to the first floor. Bypassing the vending machines, she walked down the long back corridor to the newspaper offices. By the time she reached the small newsroom, her heart was pounding.

The lights were lowered, and the place looked deserted. For a moment Thea wondered if the paper had folded after Gail's death, but from somewhere deep in the building, she could hear noises that might have been the presses running. She tried to look busy as she gazed around, wondering how she would be able to distinguish Gail's office from the rest. Hopefully it would have her name on the door or—

The yellow police tape stopped Thea cold for a moment. Her heart beat so loudly she was sure someone would hear it and come running. But all remained quiet.

Still wearing the latex gloves she'd worn to scrub toilets, she made her way across the room and tried the knob on the office. Finding it locked, she pulled a tool from her pocket and within moments, had successfully manipulated the lock. She'd done the same thing once when Nikki had locked herself in the bathroom.

Her former life was coming in handy, Thea decided as she ducked under the tape and slipped into the office. The light was off, but a window that looked out on the newsroom provided dim illumination. Another window faced the alley where the cleaning van was parked.

In a matter of seconds Thea had reconnoitered the office. There was a large desk and a computer, and beyond that, a wall of file cabinets.

She drew a deep breath. Somewhere inside here might be evidence that could either convict her or keep her free.

Her heart still racing, she reached over and closed the venetian blind at the newsroom window. The office fell into darkness, but she'd come prepared for that, too. Withdrawing a penlight from her pocket, she used the tiny beam to guide her across the office to the computer.

The series of whirs and buzzes as the machine booted up made Thea cringe. She kept glancing at the door, expecting someone to come bursting inside at any moment, demanding to know what she was doing. And then they'd call the police, and she'd be taken away—

Focus! Thea ordered herself.

Surprised and relieved that Gail Waters hadn't hidden everything behind a password, Thea searched through the complex directories and files. The sheer amount of data Waters had accumulated was both daunting and promising. It was unlikely the police had had time to even crack the surface. If they didn't know what they were looking for, they would have to go through each file with a fine-tooth comb. The work would be tedious and time-consuming, and a bored detective could easily miss a relevant piece of information.

Locating a directory that contained a massive list of names, Thea held her breath as she scrolled to the *L*'s. *Lockhart* would certainly have caught John's attention, but to Thea's relief, the name wasn't listed.

She skipped down to the *M*'s. No listing for Mancuso, either.

She even tried her maiden name and then Baltimore. Still nothing. No scanned newspaper clippings. No police report. Not one shred of evidence that Gail Waters had been looking for her.

So then why had Gail Waters been at her apartment building that day? If she hadn't been investigating Thea and Nikki's disappearance, why had she asked Mr. Dalrimple about them?

Maybe she hadn't. Maybe he'd made the whole thing up, but for what purpose? To gain Thea's trust? To use as leverage in his pursuit of her?

Maybe Dalrimple was the one who had let Waters in the night she died.

That notion conjured up all sorts of possibilities, but Thea wouldn't let herself consider them now. There was still work to do. Shutting off the computer, she aimed her light on the file cabinets. It was not unusual to keep hard copies of files, especially the more active ones. She'd required that procedure at her father's office, before his death and after, because they'd been burned one too many times by hard-drive crashes and power outages.

She opened the drawer labeled *L-M* and rifled through the files. The folders were tightly wedged together, but she scrutinized them thoroughly. She didn't see a tab for *Lockhart,* and as she moved to the *M*'s, she dropped the penlight she'd been holding between her teeth. The beam arced under the desk, out of her reach.

Suppressing an oath, Thea bent to grab for the light. And at that precise moment she heard a noise outside the office window. Someone was in the alley.

Thea froze, listening.

After a moment another sound came to her—the tinkle of shattering glass.

Someone was breaking into Gail Waters's office.

Chapter Eight

Thea reached up and closed the file drawer as quietly as she could. Then she scrambled under the desk, huddling in the tight space and praying she hadn't been seen or heard. The file cabinets were located on the same wall as the window, but in the farthest corner. It would have been difficult for anyone peering into the darkened office to see her, although the glow of her penlight might have been visible. But Thea had dropped her light… Oh, God, where was it?

Frantically she felt beneath the desk, all around her, as she heard the frame of the broken window sliding up. A cold blast of air filled the office, and then the soft telltale thump as feet landed on the carpeted floor.

Her breath suspended, Thea wondered desperately if her flashlight had rolled out on the other side of the desk, in which case, the beam would surely give her away.

The room fell into almost unbearable silence. Thea closed her eyes, straining to hear, but the only sound that reached her ears was the pounding of her heart and the muted sound of traffic outside.

She was going to be caught!

She was going to be found out. She was going to

spend the rest of her life in prison, away from Nikki—

Her hand closed over the penlight. She brought it up and almost gasped when the tiny beam caught her in the eye. She pressed the switch, dousing the light as she tried to figure out what to do.

What *could* she do?

Whoever was in this office with her hadn't come in through the front door. He'd broken in, but for what purpose?

Thea almost instantly had her answer. The intruder moved across the carpet toward the desk. Thea tried to scrunch herself into an even tighter ball. If the lights weren't turned on, if he didn't sit down and put his legs beneath the desk…

Her luck held for the moment. She heard the computer come on again, and then the familiar sounds as the system booted up. Mouse clicks followed. Then silence. Then more clicks.

He was doing exactly what she'd done. The prowler was searching for, and more than likely deleting, incriminating information.

Was he Gail Waters's killer?

Adrenaline shot through Thea's bloodstream, a heady mix of fear and excitement, undercut with an almost fatal curiosity. If she could somehow find out his identity…

Thea realized she'd been using the masculine pronoun in her mind, but she had no idea of the prowler's gender. She couldn't even see his—or her—shoes.

She turned her head, trying to get a better view. Her neck, positioned in one place for too long, creaked. The sound was like a gunshot. Thea squeezed her eyes closed, praying. For the longest moment she didn't move a muscle, and then, after an eternity, the mouse clicks started again. She could have wept with relief.

To see the intruder's shoes, she would have to move closer to the opening in the desk, crane her neck—

The door opened and the room was suddenly flooded with light. Thea almost gasped out loud, the shock was so great.

A man's voice burst across the room. ''What the hell...?''

There was a rush of movement, a loud *whack,* a masculine groan and then a thud as a body fell to the floor.

Thea held her hand over her mouth to keep from screaming. A part of her wanted to rush out from underneath the desk and see what was going on, see if she could help whoever had been hurt, but she knew that would be foolhardy, especially when she recognized the next sound—that of a clip being shoved home in a weapon. The noise took her straight back to her former life. Rick loading and unloading his gun, smiling at her all the while...

The movements of the person in the office became hurried. The computer was turned off, a file drawer opened and the contents plundered. After a moment the drawer was slammed shut again, and Thea heard the person crawl through the window and the crunch of shoes on the pavement outside, followed instantly by the sound of running footsteps.

Shaking all over, she crawled out from under the desk. The door to the newsroom was open, and light filtered in, revealing the security guard who lay motionless on the floor. Blood oozed from a gash on his left temple. Cautiously Thea approached him.

Please don't be dead, she prayed as she knelt and felt for a pulse. He was still alive, but she had no idea how badly he was hurt. Closing the office door, she hurried over to the phone and dialed 911. She gave the address of the building to the dispatcher, but when she was asked her name, she hung up.

She glanced wildly around the office. She couldn't be found here. She felt terrible leaving the security guard wounded on the floor, but what else could she do? She had to think of Nikki—

Yes, she did have to think of Nikki.

Bucking up her courage, Thea glanced around the office more carefully. Had she left anything here? Quickly she opened up the file drawer and searched through the *M*'s, making sure there wasn't a tab for Mancuso. Was it her imagination or were the folders not packed quite as tightly as they had been? Had the intruder taken a file?

Knowing she had no time for speculation, Thea slipped her light back into her pocket and turned toward the door. All she had to do now was go back upstairs and make up some excuse to Tully why the job wasn't for her. She couldn't just leave because Tully might get suspicious of her. And then when the security guard was found…

No, she had to do this the right way. She had to play it smart, which meant she couldn't afford to panic.

TULLY WAS WAITING for her in the washroom where he'd left her. He tapped his foot impatiently and glanced at his watch.

"Where the hell have you been, girl?"

"Sorry." She gave him a shaky smile. "I felt a little light-headed, so I thought I'd better get some fresh air. Guess this job is harder than I thought. All that bending over."

Tully gave her a doubtful glance. "You sure you can handle this?"

Thea opened her mouth to say, "No, I can't. You were right," when a siren sounded in the distance. Her legs started to tremble. Was it the ambulance? The police? Could she risk creating a scene with Tully? The last thing she wanted was to draw attention to herself.

"I'm sorry, Mr. Tully. Maybe I just need to pace myself. It won't happen again."

"See that it don't." He paused. "I gotta go start on the floors. You gonna be all right? Not gonna pass out or anything, are you?"

Thea felt a little guilty. She saw genuine concern in the man's eyes. "I'll be fine. Thank you, Mr. Tully."

The moment he was out of sight, she left the washroom and went in search of an office with a window that looked down on the street. An ambulance had arrived, and as she watched the paramedics unload a stretcher, two patrol cars came racing around the corner and screeched to a halt at the curb. The officers got out and started running for the building.

Escape, for the moment, was out of the question.

THE PHONE WAS RINGING when John got home. After leaving his uncle's house, he'd stopped off at Durty Nellie's, an Irish pub where a lot of cops hung out, hoping to find his brother there. He'd been trying to get in touch with Tony for days, but his brother was either buried under a heavy caseload or avoiding him. John suspected it was the latter.

He snatched up the phone, cradling it against his ear as he reached down to extract Cassandra's claws from his pants leg. "Hello?"

"That you, Johnny?"

"Yeah," he said, recognizing his partner's drawl.

Cassandra arched her back and gave him a laconic glare before stalking out to the kitchen. Her food bowl was undoubtedly empty, John thought. She always got cranky when she was hungry.

"Get your pants on, boy. We just got ourselves a lead."

Excitement rippled through John. "What's going on?"

"A buddy of mine from the Thirteenth District just called me. They've got a B and E at a newspaper office on LaSalle. Recognize the address?"

"Damn right. That's Gail Waters's paper."

"How soon can you be there?"

"I'm on my way," John told him. "You coming?"

There was a long pause. John thought he heard a woman murmuring in the background. "Nah. I'll let you take this one."

"I'll talk to you in the morning then."

John reached for his coat and holster, then glanced at his watch. He'd been home a total of three minutes. That could be a record for him.

THE AMBULANCE had already left for the hospital by the time John arrived on the scene. One of the uniforms briefed him on the security guard's condition. "He'll make it, but he's gonna have one hell of a headache in the morning."

"Was he conscious?" John asked.

"In and out."

"Could he identify the suspect? Give a description?"

The officer shrugged. "He was pretty out of it, but he said the perp was wearing a parka and a ski mask.

Beyond that, he wasn't much help. Could have been anywhere between five feet and six feet. Could have been male or female.'' The officer shrugged. ''Bradshaw's dusting for prints, but I doubt we'll find anything.''

John doubted it, too. He left the officer and walked into the building, going straight to Gail Waters's office. He and Roy had been there intermittently over the last few days, going through files, talking to Gail's coworkers. Nothing concrete had turned up, other than that she'd been very ambitious, prone to severe bouts of depression, and she might or might not have been involved with a married man.

Not much to go on, John thought, remembering the conversation with his uncle. There was still no proof she'd been murdered. Nothing but John's gut instinct.

Cold air blew in through the broken window. The office was frigid. John walked over and introduced himself to the detective on the scene.

''Mind if I have a look around?''

The detective shrugged. ''I just got here. The office was secured though, so it should be sterile.''

John nodded, then turned and observed his surroundings. The file drawers were all closed, the computer turned off, the chair shoved up against the desk. At first glance nothing appeared to be disturbed, but something was undoubtedly missing. Files? Data from the computer? Evidence he and Roy had overlooked?

He walked over to the file cabinets and glanced around, wondering which of the drawers had been opened, what had been taken from them.

''I'm going outside to have a look around,'' the detective told him. ''Holler if you find anything.''

''Sure thing.''

The detective closed the door behind him, and John studied the carpet in front of the metal cabinets. A standard white shirt button lay buried in the nap, and John bent to pick it up. Slipping the button into an evidence bag, he put it in his pocket, then opened the top drawer of the nearest cabinet to study the files, trying to detect a missing folder, a misplaced tab. Had the button come from the suspect's shirt while he stood searching through these same files?

The folders were in alphabetical order, Lambert, Lehy, Lohman and so on behind the *L* tab, and the *M*'s—Manquito, McCorkle, Morris and so forth on the *M* tab.

Wait a minute.

John's fingers backtracked. *Morris.* As in Morris Dalrimple?

The information inside was on a missing teenager from Orange County, California.

Okay, nothing there. But still, something wasn't right here. He closed the drawer slowly. A tab on one of the folders dragged against the top, as if it had been pulled out of place slightly when another file—the one in front of it or the one behind it—had been removed.

John withdrew the file and scanned the contents. The tab was labeled Manning, Frederick, but that didn't tell John much, other than to suggest the name on the missing file began with *Ma.* As John started to replace the file, he saw a photograph lying on the bottom of the drawer, as if someone had filed it in a hurry and missed the folder.

He brought it out to the light and studied it for a moment. The snapshot was of a man wearing a police uniform, but it wasn't the Chicago PD. He didn't think it was New York or L.A., either, but he couldn't be sure. The lettering on the shield was too small to make out.

He had no idea if the picture belonged to the file he'd just taken out of the drawer or to the missing file. Hell, he really had no way of knowing if a file *was* missing. But the suspect hadn't broken into Gail Waters's office and taken out a security guard for kicks. He—or she—had been looking for something, and John was willing to bet money he'd found it.

Putting the picture in the bag along with the button, he left the office. The detective was talking to one of the uniforms, but he came over to John when he saw him.

"Find anything?"

John thought about the photograph. There was something about the man's face that was strangely disturbing. "I'm not sure," he said. "I'll let you know. Let's question the cleaning crew."

THEA DECIDED she'd better make a break for it. But she'd left her coat downstairs. She tried to remember whether or not there was anything in the pockets that could be traced to her, but decided she'd better not risk it.

Even though she'd found nothing incriminating in Gail's files, the mere fact that she'd been on the premises when the office was broken into would be damning enough.

She slipped down the back hallway to the storage room, just off the alley entrance, where the cleaning crew had left their coats and gloves. As she rounded a corner, she came almost face-to-face with John.

He was talking to a man—another detective, she was sure—and Mr. Tully. She backpedaled, then flattened herself against the wall as their voices came closer. She glanced around frantically. There was a door across the hall, but she wasn't sure she could reach it without being seen. If the door was locked, she was definitely doomed.

Taking a deep breath, she dashed for the door. The knob turned in her hand and she all but fell inside. She listened at the door, trying to hear their voices again. It seemed to her that they paused right outside the door she'd just gone through, almost as if they could sense her presence.

Thea held her breath. What would she do if John suddenly opened the door and confronted her? Would she lie to him? Tell him the truth and beg for mercy?

What would *he* do?

He was a cop, she reminded herself. There was only one thing he could do. He'd have to turn her in.

She trembled as she listened to his voice. She couldn't make out what he was saying, but she'd recognize those rich tones anywhere. The sound sent a shiver of awareness rippling through her. Even as frightened as she was, she could still appreciate John's voice. The deepness of it. The sexiness of it.

She closed her eyes, remembering his kiss. Remembering how much she'd wanted it.

What is wrong with you? a little voice inside her demanded. *Why do you always pick the wrong men to fall for?*

She was an intelligent educated woman. She knew John Gallagher was dangerous to her, yet she couldn't help being drawn to him. And if she hadn't been attracted to him before, seeing him with her little girl, knowing how much he wanted to protect Nikki...

Thea drew several deep breaths, trying to steady her

nerves. He was a good man, a caring man. She had no doubt about that. But he was also a cop, sworn to uphold the law. She would be a fool to forget that.

The voices drifted away, and after a moment she chanced opening the door. She glanced up and down the hallway. The coast appeared to be clear. Stepping into the corridor, she went in search of her coat.

"GRACIOUS ME, I was becoming very worried about you," Mrs. Lewellyn said when Thea let herself into the apartment. "It's after midnight."

"I'm sorry I'm so late." Taking off her coat, Thea slung it over the back of a chair. "Thank you so much for staying with Nikki."

"I was glad to do it. But I would have felt much easier if I'd known what this mysterious trip of yours was all about." Mrs. Lewellyn studied her curiously. "I worry about you, dear. Especially with everything that's going on around here. You shouldn't be out alone so late at night."

"I can take care of myself." Thea sat down in an armchair opposite Mrs. Lewellyn and kicked off her shoes. She was suddenly exhausted, and seeing John inside that office building hadn't helped her nerves one bit. Dear God, if he'd seen her…

But he hadn't, she reminded herself. And it was all over now. She was back home safe and sound, and he never had to know where she'd been tonight. He never had to know about Baltimore, either. There was nothing for him to find in Gail Waters's files.

Mrs. Lewellyn pushed herself up from the sofa. "I'd better be getting back to my place. I'm glad you made it home, Thea dear, safe and sound," she said, echoing Thea's sentiments.

"Thanks. And thank you again for watching Nikki. I don't know what I'd do without you."

"I'm always just down the hall." At the doorway Mrs. Lewellyn turned back to her. "Oh, by the way, I see you're missing a button on your uniform. I've got a whole boxful of spares, so I'm sure we can find a match."

THEA WAS SO KEYED UP she didn't think she'd sleep a wink. After looking in on Nikki and reassuring herself that her daughter was sleeping peacefully, she stripped off all her clothes and took a long shower, hoping the hot water would relax her.

After drying her hair and pulling on a pair of worn silk pajamas, she climbed into bed. The events of the night came rushing back to her. But to her surprise, she almost immediately grew sleepy, from sheer mental fatigue, she suspected. She drowsily thought about the lack of evidence in Gail Waters's office, the intruder, the injured security guard. What did it all mean for her and Nikki?

Nothing, she hoped. Maybe this was the end of it, as far as they were concerned, and they could concentrate on the improvement Nikki had made in the past day or two.

Thea frowned. It almost seemed that Nikki's progress had begun the night Gail Waters had plunged to her death. Or was it because that was the night John Gallagher had entered their lives?

Nikki's response to him was undeniable. Thea had never known her daughter to warm to a stranger the way she had to John. With him Nikki seemed to feel safe in a way she never had with her own father. Thea wasn't even sure she herself had been able to instill that sense of security in her daughter, although she would do anything to protect her.

But John was different. There was something about him that made even Thea want to turn to him for help, made her at times want to cling to him, and she'd never been a clinger. She'd been stupid to fall for a man like Rick Mancuso, but once she'd realized her mistake, she'd set about at once to rectify it. And she'd promised herself she would never make the same mistake twice, and yet here she was, deeply attracted to a cop who had every bit as much power over her as Rick had.

Question was, would John use it against her or for her? How far would he be willing to go to protect her and her daughter?

Thea knew she would be wise not to put him to the test. In spite of Nikki's response to him, there was no place in their lives for John Gallagher. The sooner this case was closed and the sooner he walked out of their lives for good, the better.

Turning over in bed and snuggling against the pillow, Thea's last thought before she drifted off to sleep was, strangely enough, about the button missing from her uniform. Where and when had she lost it?

SHE AWAKENED SUDDENLY with a deep sense of unease. But glancing at the bedside clock, Thea realized she'd been asleep for nearly two hours. It was just after three-thirty. She had only a couple more hours before she'd have to get up and get ready for work.

Her thoughts froze as she realized suddenly what had awakened her. A sound that didn't belong in the apartment.

Thea's heart started pumping as she sat up in bed

and listened. It was probably nothing, she told herself. The building was old and creaky, and there were a lot of university students who lived here. They came home at all hours, partied long into the night.

But Thea was accustomed to the noises they made, and she knew every sound in her small apartment—the hum of the refrigerator in the kitchen, Nikki turning over in her bed, even the faint drone of the alarm clock beside her bed. She'd lain awake night after night, distinguishing the various noises, committing them to memory so that if she was ever awakened in the middle of the night by a strange sound, she'd know what to do.

Getting up as quietly as she could, she slid her feet into slippers, then padded into the tiny living room. She didn't turn on a light; she didn't need to. She could navigate the apartment in the darkness, because she'd practiced that, too.

She stood for a moment listening, almost convincing herself her overwrought nerves had conjured the sound, but then it came to her again, and she recognized almost at once what it was. The doorknob on the apartment door was turning. Someone was trying to get inside.

Crossing the room, Thea glanced out the peephole. She almost gasped in terror. The hallway lay in complete darkness, which meant someone had turned off the lights. Someone had planned this.

Panic exploded inside her. She whirled away from the door and, grabbing her coat from the back of the chair, ran toward Nikki's bedroom.

She whispered Nikki's name. Her daughter's eyes opened almost instantly. The night-light was on near Nikki's bed, and Thea reached over and pulled it from the socket. The room fell into darkness, and Nikki whimpered, reaching for Thea.

Wrapping her in a blanket, Thea gathered her daughter in her arms and hugged her tightly. "It's okay," she whispered. "We're going outside to see the snow." But she knew Nikki wasn't fooled. The child had been through too much, seen too much. She recognized terror when she saw it.

Carrying Nikki, Thea hurried back into her bedroom. A fire escape was outside the window, which had been painted shut when they'd first moved in. Thea had scraped for hours, loosening the dried paint, so she and Nikki would have an escape route. And then she'd installed a lock, hoping to keep burglars—and the Mancusos—on the outside.

But she should have known the Mancusos wouldn't resort to climbing through windows. That wasn't their style. They would come brazenly through the apartment door, every last one of them, including Rick's brothers, his father and even Lenore.

God, Lenore…

The image set Thea's hands to trembling so badly she could hardly turn the lock on the window. Finally getting it free, she slid up the sill, lifted Nikki out and then climbed out after her.

Behind her, Thea thought she heard a squeak as the apartment door opened. She gathered Nikki in her arms again and hurried down the metal steps.

Chapter Nine

The ringing of the phone jarred John from a deep sleep. He'd been dreaming about Thea, a strangely erotic dream that made him want to cover his head with a pillow and go back to sleep.

He reached out with one hand and brought the phone to his ear. "Hello?"

The caller paused. "John?"

For a moment he thought he must still be dreaming. "Who is this?"

"It's Thea."

Her voice sounded different, a mixture of reluctance and fear. John sat up in bed. "What's wrong? Is it Nikki?"

"No, she's all right. But...someone tried to break into our apartment tonight."

A chill snaked up John's spine. "Where are you? Are you both okay?"

"We're fine. We're at a phone booth on Dorchester, near the park entrance."

John was sitting on the edge of the bed by this time, cradling the phone against his shoulder as he pulled on a pair of jeans. "I remember where it is."

"The thing is..." Her voice trembled and he could

almost picture her biting her lip, trying to control her emotions. "I…we ran out of the apartment so fast I didn't bring any money. I only have the change in my pocket. I can't call a cab and we can't go back there—"

"I don't want you to go back," John broke in grimly. "Just hang tight and try to stay out of sight. I'll call dispatch as soon as we hang up and see if there's a patrol car in the area. And, Thea?"

"Yes?"

"I'm on my way."

He finished dressing in seconds and used his cell phone to call the dispatcher as he hurried out to his car.

In spite of the snowy streets, he made it to the park district in twenty minutes, heading south on Woodlawn Avenue. He took East Fifty-fourth Street to Dorchester, and as he neared the park, he spotted a cruiser sitting at the curb.

Pulling beside it John saw Thea and Nikki sitting in the back seat. Thea gazed at him through the rear glass, then leaned over and said something to Nikki.

John rolled down his window and held up his shield and ID for the officer's inspection. "I'm Gallagher," he said. "I'll take over from here."

He pulled his sedan to the curb in front of the patrol car and got out. The officer got out, too, and he and John spoke for a moment before John reached over and opened the cruiser's back door. Thea glanced up at him. Her hair was mussed, and she wasn't wearing any makeup. Her eyes were dark with worry and fear as she cradled her daughter in her arms.

"Here, let me help you," he said, and bent to take Nikki from her. The little girl whimpered, but almost immediately nestled more deeply into the blanket wrapped around her, as if she could hide deep in the folds and no one would find her.

Thea climbed out of the cruiser and followed John to his car. She'd thrown her coat over her pajamas, he noted as she slid into the front seat, and her slippers were wet from the snow. He handed her Nikki, and then reached down to slip the sodden shoes from her feet. Her skin felt like ice. He rubbed her feet for a moment, trying to restore circulation.

"I'm okay," she murmured.

"Are you sure? You don't need to go to the hospital?"

She looked alarmed. "No. No, we're fine. I just needed to get Nikki out of the cold."

John nodded, but he still wasn't convinced. He'd left the engine running. The heater was blasting warm air, but Thea was still trembling. She and Nikki huddled together as if there was nothing in the world that could separate them.

As he went around and climbed behind the wheel, a powerful emotion rose inside him. The sight of Thea and Nikki clinging to each other instilled a longing in him he couldn't explain. He wanted to be a part of their closeness, to share in the deep emotional bond that drew them together. He wanted to put his arms around both of them, protect them from whatever evil had touched their lives tonight. He wanted what he didn't think could ever be his.

Thea glanced at him, her eyes still dazed with shock and fear. "Thank you for coming so quickly. I didn't know who else to call. We ran out of the apartment so fast…" She paused, drawing a shaky breath. "Your card was in my coat pocket, and your home number was on the back. You gave it to me that first night…''

''I remember.'' He'd given it to her when they'd been standing near Gail Waters's body. John had thought then, as he did now, that Thea was a woman of mystery. His instincts had warned him she wasn't the person she professed to be, but maybe that was why he was so drawn to her. She'd been where he'd been. She'd seen what he'd seen. The darkness in his world wouldn't scare her away, because it was there in her world, too.

John wondered what had happened in her past to make her so guarded. Was she still grieving for her dead husband?

He didn't want to think about Thea with another man, even though he knew he had no right to feel possessive. They'd only shared one brief kiss. Regret whipped through him, even as he told himself he was a fool to want more.

''Can you tell me what happened tonight?'' he asked her.

Thea shrugged, shifting Nikki in her arms. The child weighed no more than a feather, but Thea was a small woman. She could use a hand now and then, whether she wanted to accept it or not.

''Why don't you put her in the seat between us?'' he suggested softly. ''That way you can buckle her in.''

Thea looked as if she wanted to protest, but then nodded. She settled Nikki in the seat between them, fastened the safety belt and then wrapped an arm around her daughter's shoulders, pulling her close. Again John felt that tugging sensation, that need to be a part of their closeness.

As Thea related the events of the night, she began

to shudder violently, and without thinking, John draped his arm over the back of the seat, his fingers barely brushing her hair.

"Why didn't you call 911?" he asked when she was finished.

A frown wrinkled her forehead. "I—I honestly didn't even think to. My first instinct was to get Nikki out of the apartment."

"Did anyone actually get into the apartment before you and Nikki escaped?"

"I think he was coming in just as we climbed out the window."

"He?"

She paused. "I just assumed..."

John shifted in the seat so that he could see her features in the streetlight. She didn't look quite as frightened as she had before, but she was still shaken. She bent and kissed the top of Nikki's head, as if to reassure herself her daughter was safe and sound beside her.

"You didn't get a look at the suspect? Didn't see a face, build, anything at all?"

"I didn't look back," Thea told him. "All I could think to do was run."

It was John's turn to pause. He stared at her for a moment longer, then pressed her. "You don't have any idea who it might have been? Think now."

She put a hand to her throat. "I don't know who it was, but I can't help wondering if maybe the break-in had something to do with...Gail Waters..." Her voice trailed off and her arm tightened around Nikki.

The little girl had been so still ever since John had carried her to the car, but now, as if sensing her mother's distress, she gazed up first at Thea and then John, her face all too knowing for someone so young.

Something twisted inside John. He turned and put the car into gear.

Thea said almost desperately, ''Where are you taking us?''

''Someplace where you'll be safe. Then I'll go back and have a look around at the apartment.''

''But...I don't have any money. And Nikki and I will need to get some clothes...''

''We'll take care of all that later,'' John told her. He glanced in the rearview mirror. The patrol car pulled out around him and then made a U-turn, heading back north. John did the same.

''What about the intruder?'' Thea asked.

''Officers were dispatched to your apartment when I called in. They'll wait for me there.''

He half expected Thea to put up more of an argument, but after a moment she turned and stared silently out the window.

They could have been killed tonight, John thought grimly. Thea and Nikki could have been killed, and there wouldn't have been a damned thing he could have done about it.

He muttered a violent oath under his breath as he headed the car toward home.

''YOU CAN PUT NIKKI to bed in the spare room,'' John said as he straightened from the fireplace. A flame leaped to life in the hearth, and he put out his hands as if to test the warmth. ''Poor kid looks beat.''

Thea sat on the sofa in John's living room with Nikki cuddled in the crook of her arm. It was strange, she thought. Nikki had been wide awake in the car, but the moment they'd gotten inside John's house, her eyes had begun to droop and her little body had gone limp. It was as if she felt safe here.

Thea felt that way, too, although she told herself it was irrational. A police detective's home was the last place she should have sought harbor. If he found out about their past, he could destroy both of their lives, but for now, Thea couldn't think beyond the moment. She was simply too exhausted.

Within a matter of moments the fire was blazing and the warmth spread into the room. Thea's chill began to dissipate. She stood and picked up Nikki, struggling a bit with the child's weight.

John said, "Here, let me—"

"No, that's okay. I've got her," Thea murmured, not wanting to relinquish her hold on her daughter. As much as she appreciated everything John had done for them, especially his kindness to Nikki, Thea knew it was time to reassert her self-reliance.

John looked as if he might protest, but then he shrugged. "Suit yourself. The guest room is back this way."

He flipped on lights as he led the way down a narrow hallway. Thea caught glimpses of a bathroom, done in royal-blue, gold and white, and a master bedroom with the lamp turned down low, casting shadows over a rumpled bed.

She knew at once that she'd gotten John up from that bed, that the sheets might still be warm from where he'd lain. The notion was disturbing and exciting at the same time.

"In here," he said, opening a door at the end of the hallway and switching on the light. It was an office of sorts with a desk and a computer, a weight bench and barbells, and a daybed covered with a patchwork quilt and blanket—and a white cat, who lifted her head at the intrusion.

It seemed incongruous to Thea that a man like John Gallagher would have a cat for a pet. A white one at that.

He picked up the feline and dumped her unceremoniously onto the carpet. "You'll be bunking on the couch tonight, Cassandra." The cat stretched, then stalked out of the room.

When John turned down the covers, Thea lay Nikki on the bed and then sat on the edge as she tucked the blanket and quilt snugly around her daughter. Nikki's dark curls spilled across the yellow pillowcase, and her mouth curved in what almost resembled a smile. She sighed deeply in her sleep, then rolled over to cuddle with her doll.

Thea glanced up at John and her heart skipped a beat. He'd been watching Nikki, too, but when he turned his gaze to Thea, the look on his face…the longing in his eyes…

No, she thought desperately. *This can't happen. I won't let it happen.*

She turned back to Nikki, smoothing the curls from her forehead and then dipping to kiss her soft cheek.

"She's a beautiful little girl," John said behind her.

Thea nodded, a lump in her throat. "I know. She's had such a hard time…" Her voice trailed away on a wave of deep emotion.

John took her arm and pulled her, very gently, to her feet. "She's safe here, Thea. I won't let anything happen to her."

"I know." *But what about me?* she wanted to ask. *How can you prevent what's happening between us?*

She walked ahead of him out the door and down the

hallway to the living room. The fire beckoned, and Thea, still bundled in her coat, went to stand in front of the hearth. John had gone into the kitchen to make coffee, and she used the moment to gaze around.

The house was small, a post-Second World War bungalow that looked as if it had been recently refurbished. The oak floors had been stripped and refinished, the warm hues of the wood accentuated by throw rugs. The furniture was comfortable, the thick cushions upholstered in a durable yet attractive fabric in earth tones. A leather recliner had been positioned near the fireplace, and Thea could picture John kicking back after a double shift, perhaps even dozing in front of the fire.

There were pictures on the walls, prints of sailboats on Lake Michigan and framed snapshots of men and women and boys and girls Thea assumed were all members of John's family. But the arrangement of the photographs lacked symmetry, as if some of the pictures had been taken down and not replaced. Thea couldn't help wondering who the subject had been in the missing photos.

Lamplight cast a warm glow over the room. It was not at all the sort of home Thea would have expected of a bachelor, and with something of a shock, she realized she'd never asked John if he was married. Was that the reason his house was so homey? Was there a Mrs. Gallagher lurking somewhere nearby?

The thought made Thea distinctly uncomfortable. A prickle of something she wanted to deny shot through her, and for a moment she wished she'd never called John tonight. She wished she'd never met him, because now that she had, it was going to be a very long time before she forgot him.

He picked that moment to enter the room, his presence filling the small cozy area. He carried two mugs of coffee by the handles in one hand and, in the other, a woman's silk apricot robe.

Thea's heart began to pound at the sight of that robe. Who did it belong to…and where was the owner?

He set the mugs of coffee on the small table near the recliner and handed the robe to Thea. "This should fit. You're probably starting to get a little warm in that coat."

"I hadn't even thought about it," Thea murmured, but now that he'd mentioned it, she was very warm indeed. She took the robe reluctantly, fingering the silky fabric.

"It belonged to my ex-wife," he explained as if reading her mind.

Thea lifted her gaze to meet his. "Are you sure she won't mind my wearing it?"

He shrugged. "She's got a new husband and a new baby to worry about. I seriously doubt she'll be coming back for her robe."

Was that hurt in his voice? Thea wondered. Or merely irony?

She slipped out of her coat and into the robe, belting it around her waist. John took her coat and tossed it over the back of the couch. Turning, he picked up the mugs and handed her one. "Here. I thought you could use a cup of coffee. I know I can. It's decaf, by the way."

"Thanks." Thea cradled the steaming mug in both hands. She turned toward the fire, gazing into the flames. "How long were you married?"

"A few years. We've been divorced two. How about you?"

She glanced at him, startled. "Me?"

"How long were you married when Nikki's father died?" Firelight flickered in his eyes, looking like tiny flames of...what? Passion?

Thea shivered. "We were divorced when he died. We had been for years."

It was John's turn to be surprised. "His death must have hit Nikki pretty hard. I guess they were close."

Thea closed her eyes briefly. How could she explain Rick's relationship with Nikki? He'd never loved their daughter. She'd been merely a tool for him to use against Thea. A possession his mother had coveted. A Mancuso to be trained in the art of corruption.

Thea rubbed her face, suddenly wearier than she could ever remember being.

"I don't mean to pry," John said. He set down his mug and turned to Thea. His blue gaze was very intense. Another shiver ripped through her as her stomach fluttered in awareness.

"You look tired." He lifted his hand to tuck a curl behind her ear. His touch made her tremble, made her knees threaten to buckle. The rush of adrenaline she'd experienced earlier was a dangerous thing, because the aftermath could sometimes be a powerful aphrodisiac. Thea knew she could be in big trouble tonight if she didn't keep her distance.

She smothered a yawn. "I do feel tired."

"You can take my bed. Try to get some sleep while I'm gone."

He was no longer touching her, and Thea felt bereft. "Where are you going?"

"To your apartment."

She felt the panic well up in her again. Part of her alarm had to do with the fear she'd experienced earlier, but another part had to do with what John might find there—if the intruder hadn't found it first. She'd left her stash there, the money she and Nikki would need if they should have to run. And it was beginning to look as if they might.

She said softly, "Do you have to go tonight? Maybe Nikki and I could go with you when she wakes up."

He gazed down at her, frowning. "I don't think that's a good idea. Do you really want to take her back there? You're both safe here."

"But we can't stay here indefinitely." She folded her arms and gazed into the fire. "I have to go to work."

"I know," John agreed as he turned toward the front door. "But until I can figure out what the hell is going on in that apartment building, I'll do whatever it takes to keep you and Nikki from going back there."

THE OFFICERS who had answered the call were still on the scene when John arrived, but they were getting impatient.

"We were told to wait for you," one of them said, "but we were beginning to think you weren't going to show."

John shrugged in response. "So what did you find?"

"No tool marks on the door, but it was unlocked when we got here. The window in one of the bedrooms was open, as well. The suspect might have gotten out that way."

John had a sudden vision of Thea and Nikki going through the window, climbing down the slippery stairs, running through the darkened streets...

"Either the suspect was one helluva locksmith or he had a key," the other officer said.

"What about the light in the hallway?" It had been

on when John arrived, but Thea had said it was turned off earlier.

"We found it on," the first officer replied. "The hall and outside lights are controlled by a panel in the basement. Someone could have flipped the switch, but he would've had to know in advance where the control panel was located."

"Aren't most of them located in the basement?" John asked.

"Probably," the officer conceded. "Nothing appears to be disturbed in here, but you'll have to get the tenant to go through the contents to make certain. There's not much else we can do."

John nodded. "Okay. You can take off. I'm going to stay and have another look around."

After the officers had departed, John prowled the living room and kitchen, trying to get a feel for anything missing. But he'd only been in Thea's apartment twice before, and each time he might have been a little more preoccupied with her than was warranted. Still, his powers of observation were pretty keen, and so far he couldn't spot anything out of place.

He checked the bathroom and Nikki's bedroom before walking into Thea's room. Even though he had every right to be there, his presence in her bedroom still seemed a little like an invasion of privacy. The room was tiny. She'd given Nikki the larger bedroom, probably because she would have been worried about the window in this room opening onto a fire escape.

He gazed at the articles on top of her dresser—a hairbrush and comb, makeup, a small vial of perfume. He resisted the urge to remove the stopper from the bottle and inhale the scent. Turning, he scanned the room. The bed was unmade. He could imagine the covers had been hastily kicked aside when she'd been awakened by the noise at the front door.

A cramped closet revealed a few articles of clothing, two clean uniforms, three pairs of shoes—flats, heels and walking shoes—and a large suitcase.

John frowned at the sight of the bag. It wasn't tucked away into the back corner of the closet or stored out of the way on the top shelf. Instead, it rested on the floor near the front of the closet, within easy reach of the door.

Unable to resist, John knelt and laid the suitcase on its side, but the snaps were locked into place. Unless he wanted to break the latches, the contents would have to remain a mystery. He picked up the case, testing its weight, as he returned it to its original position.

Why would Thea have a packed suitcase in her closet? Was she using the bag for storage? Was she planning a trip?

One of her pink uniforms lay on the bedroom floor where it had apparently fallen from the back of a chair. Either Thea had knocked it off in her haste to flee the apartment, or the suspect had been in this room, too.

John was almost sure of the latter. The room carried a subtle fragrance, a lingering odor that didn't seem to belong to Thea. It was a masculine scent, John thought, but then again, maybe that was purely his imagination. B-and-E perpetrators were usually male, so maybe the statistics were coloring his judgment.

He stooped to pick up the uniform, and as he placed it on the back of the chair, he saw that a button was missing from the front. A dark suspicion crept over him as he stared down at the uniform.

Tully, the head of the cleaning crew at the building that housed the *Press,* had said there was a new woman with them that night, someone the owner had supposedly sent over. A woman who had, apparently, left before she could be questioned. A woman Tully described as petite with short dark hair.

Thea?

He withdrew the plastic evidence bag from his coat pocket. The button in the bag was exactly the same as the buttons on the uniform.

He should have already turned the button in. Removing evidence from a crime scene without reporting it was a serious violation, but for some reason John had kept the button and the picture he'd found in Gail Waters's office. It suddenly hit him why he might have done so. Had he subconsciously recognized that button? Had a part of him suspected it was Thea's?

So what in hell had she been doing in Waters's office? Had she assaulted the security guard? Had she tried to kill him?

John felt slightly ill as he turned toward the window. The officers had closed it earlier, but he slid it up again, letting the cold air rush over him. What in hell was going on here? Who was Thea Lockhart really, and what kind of fool was she playing him for?

Down on the street a man stood beneath a streetlight, gazing up at the window where John stood. He recognized the dark parka almost at once. So Fischer was finally ready to make contact.

John climbed out the window and clambered down the fire escape. He half expected the informant to have vanished by the time he got to the ground, but a movement in the alley behind him told him otherwise. He pulled out his weapon just in case.

The alley was cut off from the streetlights, and the

shadows from the buildings on either side made it almost pitch-black. John walked slowly forward.

"You won't need the gun," the man said from the darkness. "You should know that by now." As always, there was something odd about Fischer's voice, as if he was deliberately trying to disguise it. He moved forward slightly, allowing John to make him out. "It's good to see you again, John."

John squinted in the darkness. "I've been seeing you around the past few days. I was wondering when you'd make contact."

"Didn't have anything to contact you about," the man said. He eased back into the shadows a bit.

"And now you do?"

"I don't have any information for you," Fischer clarified. "Just a few observations."

John fought back his impatience. Observations he didn't need, but he also couldn't afford to alienate a valuable informant. "Let's hear them."

"What do you know about Gail Waters?" Fischer asked him.

John shrugged. "She was a reporter for a small paper called the *Press*. She also coproduced a local cable show called *Vanished!*"

"The natural assumption would be that her murder—if she was murdered—had something to do with one of her investigations," Fischer said. "Maybe she found someone who didn't want to be found."

John shrugged. "That would be the natural assumption, sure. Are you saying that's a false assumption?"

The informant paused. "You have a vested interest in this case, John. She was investigating your own father's disappearance at the time of her death, wasn't she?"

John frowned, straining to see through the gloom. "How do you know that?"

"Informants are like reporters. We don't give away our sources."

"All right," John said, no longer bothering to hide his impatience. "What's your point?"

"Suppose her death had nothing to do with any of her investigations. At least not directly."

"Go on."

"You would have been looking in the wrong direction all this time. Maybe you were even steered in that direction. Her investigations could have been a smoke screen."

The conversation with his uncle the night before came back to John. Liam had warned him that his brother could become a suspect in Ashley's murder if the investigation into Gail Waters's death became public. But was Liam really worried about Tony—or someone else?

"If you dig deep enough, you might find Gail's private life as interesting as her professional," the informant said.

"There was a rumor at the paper that she was involved with a married man," John told him.

"If he was someone important, someone in a position of power, say, then he might have been willing to do something drastic to keep their relationship from becoming public."

"You talk as if you know who he is," John said.

"All I have are suspicions." The informant paused. "But if my suspicions are right, this investigation could get you in serious trouble. It could take you places you don't want to go.''

"I'm beginning to realize that.'' John shoved his hands deep into the pockets of his coat. He was suddenly very cold.

Chapter Ten

When Thea awakened, a glimmer of sunlight drifted through the closed blinds at the window, and for a moment she couldn't remember where she was or how she'd gotten there. She sat up on the sofa in a panic, gazing around her strange surroundings as the events of the night came rushing back to her.

Nikki! Where was her baby?

Throwing off the afghan that had been covering her, Thea jumped to her feet and raced down the hallway to the guest room. The door was ajar. She opened it wider and looked in.

Nikki was still asleep, the white cat curled up at her feet. They both looked so peaceful. Thea stood watching them for a moment, wishing it could be like this always. She'd even managed to catch a few hours of sleep herself after John had left, although she'd told herself she was only going to stretch out on the couch for a few minutes.

Somehow she hadn't been able to bring herself to crawl into John's bed. Lying where he lay, dreaming where he dreamed, would have been too intimate and much too disturbing.

Even being in his home was a danger Thea should

have avoided. She felt closer to him here and even more drawn to him, almost as if by observing where he lived, she had a deeper insight into the man. And she liked what she saw, Thea had to admit. She liked it very much.

No good can come of this, she warned herself as she backed out of the guest room and pulled the door closed. The sooner she could find a way to get Nikki and herself safely away from here, the better for all of them. The last thing John needed was to get mixed up in her problems. If he learned the truth about her, he would have two options—turn her in or turn against everything he believed in.

Thea knew instinctively he was an honest cop, one of the good guys. It wouldn't be easy for him to look the other way. It wouldn't be easy for her to ask him to.

But until she could get back to her apartment and get her money and IDs, Thea only had one option. Stay here and risk detection with every minute that passed on the clock.

The smell of coffee drew her to the kitchen, but John was nowhere in sight. A note lay on the counter near the coffeemaker, and as Thea picked it up, something fell from the paper and rolled across the countertop.

She stared at the white button, a warning flashing somewhere inside her. Mrs. Lewellyn's words the night before came flowing back to her. *Oh, by the way, I can see you're missing a button on your uniform.*

Thea had just gotten home from Gail Waters's office. Was it possible…?

Her heart pounded in her ears. Dear God, what if John had found the button at that office? What if he knew now that she had been there? Would he arrest her for Waters's murder? Was he out there right now, looking for the proof he needed to put her away?

With shaking fingers, she unfolded the note and read the words he'd scrawled across the paper.

Thea and Nikki—
Plenty of food in the fridge so help yourselves. Don't worry about dinner tonight. I'll try to be home early, and I'll bring something when I come. Stay inside and keep the doors locked. I'll take care of your job. Think of Nikki, Thea. She's safe where you are.

Was that last line a warning? Thea wondered. Did he somehow know her first instinct when she found the button would be to run?

But what if he was testing her? Maybe he was only guessing that the button belonged to her. If she ran, wouldn't that prove his suspicions?

Thea's head whirled with indecision, and when the phone rang she almost jumped out of her skin. She didn't answer it, but waited for the machine to pick up. When she heard John's voice, her heart began to hammer in slow painful thuds against her chest.

"Thea? Pick up if you're there. And you'd better be there," he added in a low ominous tone. Or was that her imagination?

She reached for the phone and brought the receiver to her ear. "Hello?" Her voice sounded calm enough. She drew a long breath, trying to steady her racing pulse.

"Thea? Is everything all right?"

Thea tried to detect a double meaning in his question. He did sound guarded. That wasn't her imagination, she was sure of it. "Yes, we're fine. I didn't hear you come in earlier."

"You were sleeping so soundly I didn't want to wake you. So was Nikki." He paused, almost as if he was expecting her to jump in and explain about the button. When she remained silent he said, "The reason I called is to warn you—"

Thea gasped in spite of herself. *"Warn me?"*

Another pause. "Yes. My sister, Fiona, is coming over this morning. I asked her to bring you and Nikki some things I thought you might need."

Thea's knees almost buckled with relief. "That was thoughtful of you. But I really need to get back to my apartment today. I have to get back to work." And Nikki would be safe at her preschool. The facilities were excellent.

"I've already called the diner and told them you need some time off," John told her. "Your employer was very understanding."

Thea frowned. It wasn't his place to ask her employer to give her time off. That was something Rick would have done.

But even as she had that thought, Thea knew exactly what she was doing. She was trying to vilify John, even in a small way, so that she wouldn't be tempted to trust him, to confide in him, to ask him for help.

She closed her eyes as another wave of panic washed over her. What was it about John Gallagher that made her want to risk everything? If she only had herself to be concerned with, she might have gone to him. She might have told him everything. But there was Nikki to consider. Nikki's future she had to protect. If she went to jail, John could do nothing to keep Nikki from Lenore Mancuso.

"Fiona has red hair," John was saying. "Tall, skinny, freckles across her nose. Make her show you her ID before you let her in if you're not absolutely positive it's her."

"All right," Thea agreed.

"I guess that's it. I'll see you and Nikki tonight."

"Thank you for everything, John," she said, and meant it.

He fell silent and then, after a moment, "Don't leave, Thea."

Was that a warning note or a plea in his voice? Thea wished she knew.

JOHN HAD JUST GOTTEN BACK from dropping the picture he'd found in Gail Waters's office at the lab when Roy Cox came in with a package.

"What's that?"

"The 911 tape you requested this morning." Roy tossed the padded envelope at John, then sat down behind his desk and propped up his feet.

"That was fast," John said, breaking the seal on the envelope.

"We aim to please," Roy drawled. "So what did I miss last night?"

John filled him in on what had happened at Gail Waters's office while he snapped the copy of the 911 tape into a cassette player. Pressing the play button, he located the time and the call he was interested in on the accompanying transcript, then fast-forwarded.

The moment he heard the woman's voice after the dispatcher had answered the call, John's heart took a nosedive. There was no question in his mind about the identity of the caller, even though her voice had sounded strained, almost garbled. The woman who had placed the 911 call from Waters's office was Thea.

So where did he go from here? Should he haul her in for questioning? Treat her as he would any other suspect?

His good sense told him that was exactly what he should do. To hold back now, to sweep the evidence he'd found against her under the rug was to do exactly what he'd accused his uncle of doing. John had never been one to look the other way. He'd never been one to shy away from his duty, even when his responsibilities had put him at odds with his own family.

So why was he holding back now? Why was he protecting Thea when to do so meant risking his job?

This was the danger in getting involved with a suspect. He'd seen other cops fall victim to a beguiling predator, seen them lose their careers, their families, everything for the sake of a woman whose sole interest was saving her own skin. John had never figured himself to be one of those cops. He'd had a bad marriage, sure, but Meredith had been basically good. She'd been the right sort of woman, while Thea—

"What the hell's the matter with you?" Roy demanded. "You look like you just swallowed a june bug."

Without a word John ejected the tape from the machine, then slipped it back into the envelope and locked it in his desk drawer.

Roy said, "Didn't you hear me? What's on that tape that's got you so wired?"

"Nothing," John told him.

"Right." Roy paused, then said, "You wouldn't be holding out on me, would you, partner?"

John shrugged. "I'm working on a couple of leads. I'll let you know if they pan out."

"You do that." Roy twirled the ends of his handlebar mustache as he studied John curiously. Roy looked, all of a sudden, like the cat who had swallowed the canary, and John couldn't help wondering why.

THEA PEERED through the peephole in John's front door at the redhead who stood on the porch. From what Thea could see, the woman was tall and thin, but from the distorted view through the peephole, Thea couldn't detect the freckles.

Opening the door a fraction, Thea said, "Yes?"

The woman smiled at her. She was very attractive, in a flamboyant sort of way, with her thick curly red hair and brilliant blue eyes. She smiled at Thea, holding up a department-store shopping bag. "I'm Fiona, John's sister. He said you'd be expecting me."

Thea paused, drawn to the woman's friendly face, but she knew to be cautious, even without John's warning. "He said I should make you show me your ID," she said apologetically.

The redhead laughed good-naturedly. "That sounds like John. Always protective." She set down the shopping bag and fished in her shoulder bag for her wallet, then held up her driver's license. "Fiona Colleen Gallagher," she said, giving Thea a wry look. "Can you get any more Irish than that?"

The name suited her red hair, Thea decided, as she opened the door to let Fiona enter. The scent of jasmine filled the air as John's sister strode with familiar ease into the living room.

Nikki was sitting in front of the fire, drawing in a notebook Thea had found for her in the kitchen. There were no toys in John's house, nothing with which to occupy a four-year-old child, even one as quiet as Nikki. But she wasn't complaining. Gripping a pencil tightly in her fist, she concentrated on the picture she was drawing, not even glancing up when Fiona came into the room.

"This must be Nikki." Fiona's voice was soft and lyrical. She didn't look anything like John. The only resemblance Thea could detect was their blue eyes.

Fiona slipped out of her coat, revealing black pants and a black turtleneck sweater. She looked very chic, and by comparison, Thea felt dowdy in pajamas and a robe. It was the middle of the morning. She didn't like not being able to get dressed.

Fiona sat down on the hearth near Nikki, but not so close that she would alarm her. Nikki glanced up, curiosity getting the better of her, then ducked her head back down to her drawing.

"I have something for you," Fiona said to the little girl. "John told me how much you love to color. I can see that you're quite an artist, too." She pulled a coloring book and a box of crayons from her shopping bag and lay them on the floor near Nikki. "I've brought you some games, too, some of my all-time favorites. I'll teach you how to play if you like."

Nikki still didn't react, but she inched closer to the crayons.

Thea said, "That was very thoughtful of you, Fiona. Thank you so much."

The redhead shrugged. "Don't mention it. John told me a little about you and Nikki." Her gaze met Thea's, and sympathy flashed through her eyes before she quickly subdued it. "Anyway, he called and asked me to pick up a few things he thought the two of you might need. He…sort of described you, and I guessed at your sizes. I hope everything fits.''

''You didn't have to go shopping for us,'' Thea said. ''I could have gone home and gotten everything we needed.''

''John didn't seem to like that idea. Anyway, he gave me carte blanche, so I went to Marshall Field's. That'll teach him.'' Her smile was so charming, Thea couldn't help but relax around her. ''Would you like to go get dressed? I can stay out here with Nikki.''

''I wouldn't want to impose,'' Thea murmured, trying to gauge her daughter's reaction. Nikki had abandoned her drawing for the coloring book and crayons. She seemed oblivious to both Thea and Fiona. ''If you're sure you don't mind.''

''Of course not. Take your time.'' Fiona handed Thea the shopping bag, and as Thea headed for the bathroom, she heard the redhead talking to Nikki in her soft musical voice.

John had told Thea that his brothers were all police officers, but he'd never mentioned what his sister did for a living. Was she a cop, too? Was that why she was here? To try to extract information from her?

She scolded herself for her suspicions, but Thea knew she had every right to be cautious. If John had found the button from her uniform in Gail Waters's office, his suspicions would be deeply aroused.

Taking a quick shower and drying off, Thea found everything she needed in the bag, including toiletries and even lipstick and mascara. Pulling on a pair of beautifully tailored gray slacks and a cream sweater— the kind of clothes she'd once taken for granted—she felt less vulnerable. She hurried back out to find Fiona and Nikki engaged in a friendly game of Chutes and

Ladders. The redhead clapped enthusiastically when Nikki made a strategic move.

"You've played this before, I can see," Fiona told her.

"We used to play it all the time," Thea said. But Nikki had lost interest in almost everything except coloring and her doll after that terrible night. But all of a sudden she seemed to be making a remarkable recovery. What was it about the Gallaghers that drew Nikki out of her shell? What was it about John—and now his sister—that made Thea yearn for the closeness she'd once shared with her father and Mona?

John Gallagher was exactly the kind of man Thea's father would have wanted for her. Strong, protective, but with an innate goodness that made him the antithesis of Rick. But it was that innate goodness, that strong sense of right and wrong, that made him so dangerous to her now.

After they finished their game, Fiona got up from the floor and sat on the sofa beside Thea. "So tell me what's going on between you and my brother," she said bluntly.

Thea glanced at her in shock. "I...don't know what you mean. Surely he must have told you what happened, why Nikki and I are here."

Fiona shrugged. "John's the strong silent type, but I guess you've probably figured that out for yourself."

When Thea didn't comment, Fiona went on, "Nick, my middle brother, is the hothead, and Tony, the youngest, is the loner. The Gallaghers have managed to produce all the stereotypes, and throw in the fact that we're Irish, stubborn and opinionated as hell, you've got a real bloodbath at family gatherings."

Thea smiled. "I'll bet it's not as bad as all that."

"We have our moments." Fiona's expression clouded briefly, then she brightened. "Why don't you get John to bring you and Nikki over tomorrow night? You can see for yourself."

"Tomorrow night?" There was a distinct possibility Thea and Nikki wouldn't be anywhere near Chicago tomorrow night.

"My mother's throwing a retirement party for one of the captains on the force. He was one of my father's best friends, so the whole family will be there, along with a good portion of the Chicago Police Department."

The very thought of being in a roomful of cops was more than a little unnerving. Thea managed a polite smile. "Thanks. That's very nice of you."

"You may not think so once you're there. It's not unusual to have a brawl when my brothers and cousins get together. Especially if my cousin, Kaitlin, and her husband show."

She seemed to expect a response, so Thea inquired mildly, "There's a family problem?"

Fiona rolled her eyes. "It's so stupid. Have you ever heard the story of the Hatfields and the McCoys?"

"Of course." Thea watched Nikki for a moment, her thoughts more on her and her daughter's predicament than on what Fiona was telling her.

"My family has been embroiled in a ridiculous feud for over seventy years. The Gallaghers and the O'Roarke's," she said dramatically, then immediately sobered. "There's even been bloodshed."

"What happened?" Thea asked, interested in spite of herself.

Fiona settled back against the cushions, gazing at the fire. She told the story as if she'd heard it a million times before. "My grandfather, William Gallagher, came over from Ireland with his best friend, James O'Roarke, when the two of them were just teenagers. They were like brothers—until they both fell in love with the same woman.

"The rivalry made them bitter enemies. When Colleen—my grandmother—fell in love with James O'Roarke, it broke my grandfather's heart. He joined the Chicago Police Department while James turned to the other side of the law. He made a fortune bootlegging, sort of an Irish Al Capone, and when my grandmother found out what he was up to, she broke off their engagement. She eventually married my grandfather."

"Sounds very romantic," Thea said, but she couldn't help wondering why Fiona was telling her all this. What did it have to do with her?

"Not really," Fiona said sadly. "I don't think my grandmother ever got over her love for James, and my grandfather hated him even more because of it. He made it his life's work to bring down the O'Roarkes, and the bitterness between the two families has continued over the years. My brother Nick has always been convinced that an O'Roarke killed our father, even though Dad's body was never found."

Thea glanced at her in surprise. "Your father's body was never found?"

Fiona shook her head. "He left for a fishing trip one Friday afternoon, and we never saw him again."

John's father had disappeared. Thea's heart began to beat a painful tattoo. She wasn't sure yet of the significance of this revelation, but somehow she knew it was important, knew it might be connected to Gail Waters.

"Anyway," Fiona continued, "to make a long story

even longer, my cousin Kaitlin committed the unpardonable sin of marrying an O'Roarke. Even though her husband, Dylan, is a great guy, my Uncle Liam has basically disowned his daughter. I feel sorry for them both, only—'' Fiona's tone became wistful ''—I do sometimes wonder what it would be like to love someone so much you'd defy both your families to be together.''

Thea wondered what that kind of love would be like, too, and unaccountably, she thought of John. What would he do if he found out the truth about her past? Would he defy the law to protect her? Would he turn against his own family, the brotherhood of cops who stood together through thick and thin?

Why would he? He wasn't in love with her any more than she was in love with him. They'd met less than a week ago, and if she'd learned anything during her painful marriage to Rick, it was that only fools rush in.

''I can't thank you enough for everything you've done for us,'' Thea said warmly. She gazed down at her slacks and sweater. The size was nearly perfect. ''But…I wonder if I could ask another favor of you.''

''Name it,'' Fiona said. ''I've got the rest of the day off, and I don't have anything planned for another—'' she glanced at her watch ''—three hours or so.''

''It shouldn't take that long,'' Thea told her. ''I need to go out for a while, run an errand that can't wait until John gets home. Would you look after Nikki for me? I'll be back as fast as I can.''

''Well, sure, but didn't John want you to stay put?''

''This won't take long.''

Fiona shrugged. ''I don't mind staying with Nikki. In fact, I'd adore it.'' She reached in her purse and pulled out some bills. "Here. Won't you need money for a cab?"

"I can take the El."

Fiona got up and tucked the money into Thea's coat pocket. "Take a cab. It'll be faster, and besides, I'll add it to John's tab."

JOHN COULDN'T GET that 911 tape out of his mind all morning. If he hadn't found the white button in Gail Waters's office last night and if he hadn't found out a button was missing from one of Thea's uniforms, he might not have recognized her voice on the tape. She'd only said a few words and her voice was very rushed and muffled, but considering everything else, he had very little doubt that it was Thea. She'd been in Gail Waters's office the night before, but why? What had she been looking for?

He shouldn't be so surprised, John thought as he drove along Lake Shore Drive. From the moment he'd first laid eyes on her, he'd known she was hiding something. Now he had to figure out what that something was—and what it had to do with Gail's death.

But even after finding the button and hearing her voice on the tape, John still had a hard time thinking of Thea as a suspect. He'd been a cop long enough to know there was no set MO for murderers, and he sure as hell knew that appearances could be deceiving. Just because Thea was small and a female didn't mean she couldn't have been on the roof that night. She could have taken Gail by surprise, pushed her from behind. Hell, anything was possible.

But a murderer? Somehow John couldn't make himself believe it, and he realized his qualms had less to do with her physical appearance and more to do with his growing feelings for her. He didn't want to believe her capable of murder. He didn't want to think he could be that taken in by someone, but it happened all the time. Cops could be gullible, too.

He found a parking space near Baxter House, the luxury lakeside high-rise where Superintendent Dawson lived—or had, until he and his wife split up. Flashing his shield and ID to the doorman, John rode the elevator up to the ninth floor and then made his way to the unit at the far end of the hallway.

He rang the bell, then glanced around as he waited for someone to answer. The carpet in the hallway was a plush silvery gray, so thick his footsteps had been completely muted. Oil paintings hung along the corridor, adorning the spaces over antique tables and fresh flower arrangements in crystal vases.

It was a far cry from the old neighborhood, John thought, an image suddenly popping into his head of the house where the Dawsons had once resided, two doors down from the house John's mother and grandmother still lived in.

There'd been flowers there, too, but not the white artful arrangements gracing this elegant hallway. Anncttc Dawson had been partial to geraniums back then, he remembered. Her window boxes had always been the most colorful in the neighborhood. But after Ashley's murder, Mrs. Dawson had let the flowers wither and die, and soon after, the family had moved away.

When the door was finally answered, John saw a look of shock flash across the woman's face, followed quickly by a look of alarm. Annette Dawson was a tall thin woman who had once been very attractive, but the years following her daughter's murder had not been kind to her. Her face was heavily lined in spite of the camouflage of makeup, and her blond hair was streaked with gray.

"John? John Gallagher?"

He smiled. "Hello, Mrs. Dawson. It's been a while, hasn't it?"

"I can't even remember the last time I saw you." She rested her hand on the door frame. John noticed she wasn't wearing a wedding ring. "It must have been Robert Keaton's retirement party. Or maybe Dave Torrey's."

"May I come in?" John asked politely. "I won't take up much of your time."

She hesitated, then moved back for him to enter. Leading him into an almost entirely white living room, she motioned toward an elegant sofa. John was almost afraid to sit on it. He perched on the edge, watching Mrs. Dawson as she gravitated toward the ornate fireplace. There were logs in the grate, but the fire wasn't lit. She didn't seem to notice as she stood with her back to the hearth.

"So what's this about, John? Or should I call you Detective? I assume you're here in a professional capacity."

He nodded. "I need to ask you some questions about your stepson, Eddie."

Her fingers fluttered upward to trace the smooth swirl of her hair. "What about him?"

"I have reason to believe he's living in the building where a woman died recently. You probably heard about it on TV. The victim was a local reporter." John watched the emotions flicker across her face—fear, anger, determination. He wondered what they all meant. "I'd like for you to give me his address."

"Why?" she said coldly.

He lifted a brow at her tone. "Because I'm investigating the case and I want to ask him some questions."

"I understood that woman's death was a suicide. Why would you need to talk to Eddie about that?" Her gaze was almost hostile now, and John knew he was putting his career on the line by even coming here.

His uncle had warned him that he was treading on very dangerous ground, and now, as he watched the anger flash in Annette Dawson's gray eyes, he realized what he was up against. She was still the superintendent's wife, and by coming here, he had put himself on the outside. He'd pitted himself against the Brotherhood.

We take care of our own. That's how it works.

"Look, Mrs. Dawson, you and my mother have been friends for a long time. I don't like coming here, but I wouldn't be doing my job if I didn't. I'm going to ask you again where I can find Eddie."

He thought for a moment she wasn't going to answer, then she shrugged. "He's been estranged from the family for years. I don't know where he is."

"I think you do," John said bluntly.

She gazed at him coldly, her demeanor one of haughty aloofness, and then she seemed to crumble before his very eyes. Her shoulders slumped and she crossed to a brocade armchair and sat. Her hands gripped the carved wood so tightly her knuckles whitened. "I'm sure you've heard that my husband and I are separated."

"I'm sorry," he said noncommittally.

"Things haven't been right with our family since Ashley's death."

"It's been rough for a lot of people," John said.

She nodded. "I don't want to have to live through

that again. After all these years I don't want to see Ashley's name splashed across the front pages again. I don't want to have to view those ghastly pictures. Is it too much to ask that my child be allowed to rest in peace?"

"I understand how you feel. But Ashley's murderer is sitting on death row at this very minute. Doesn't Gail Waters deserve the same justice?"

"She got what she deserved."

"I beg your pardon?" John couldn't believe what he'd just heard.

Suddenly the anger and coldness were back. Annette lifted her chin and glared at him. "She had no right prying into my family's private matters, and neither do you, Detective. If my husband finds out you've been here, there'll be hell to pay. You know that, don't you?"

John shrugged. "I'm just trying to do my job. I have reason to believe that Eddie may have seen Gail Waters on the night she died. I'm not accusing him of anything, but I need to talk to him about it. It's standard procedure. I also have a feeling Gail Waters may have talked to you, Mrs. Dawson."

She almost smiled, a bitter twisting of her lips. "Our paths may have crossed once or twice. I really can't recall."

She was lying, John thought. Annette Dawson had undoubtedly talked to Gail Waters, but after his conversation with Fischer last night, John was no longer convinced Ashley's murder had been the topic. Was it possible Gail Waters had been the reason for the Dawsons' breakup? She'd been young, beautiful and, from everything John had learned about her, very ambitious. Superintendent Dawson could have given her entry into a lot of important circles, but…suppose he'd refused? Suppose Gail had turned to blackmail?

What the hell had he landed in the middle of here? John wondered as he left Annette Dawson's apartment. Did he really believe that Ed Dawson or his wife could have been involved in Gail Waters's death?

And why, all of a sudden, was either scenario easier to swallow than the thought of Thea's involvement?

THEA KEPT A SPARE KEY to her apartment in the pocket of her coat, in case her purse was ever snatched on the train or on the street—which had happened to her once. She let herself into the building, then glanced over her shoulder to make sure she hadn't been followed. The last thing she needed was for John to find her here. He'd demand to know why she'd come back to the apartment, demand an explanation for how a button from her uniform had gotten into Gail Waters's office.

It was possible, of course, that he hadn't found the button at the newspaper office. It was possible he was grasping at straws. But the last thing she wanted to do was fuel his suspicions, at least until she could get the money she'd hidden in her apartment, along with another set of fake IDs and Nikki's real birth certificate.

It had probably been a mistake, keeping anything from their past, but somehow Thea hadn't been able to leave behind proof of Nikki's parentage. What if the Mancusos had someone kidnap Nikki and whisk her off to a foreign country? How could she prove the child was hers?

Still, it had been a gamble, but her whole life had become one big risk. What she had to do and do well was play the odds.

She started up the stairs, but voices somewhere on

the second floor stopped her. Someone slammed a door and then footsteps strode down the corridor toward the stairs. Thea backed down the steps and tried to plaster herself against the wall, hoping to remain unseen, because one of the voices had sounded a little like John's.

The man was coming down the stairs now. He would see her when he rounded the landing and headed down the second set of steps. Thea turned her back to the stairs and leaned against an apartment door, pretending to insert a key into the lock.

The steps slowed near the bottom, and Thea knew he had spotted her. She almost expected to hear him call her name or feel his hand on her arm. Wiggling the knob as if dealing with a stubborn lock, she almost gasped when the door opened. She had no choice but to go inside.

Keeping her face averted from the man on the stairs, she closed the door, but then opened it a crack to see when the coast was clear. The man had paused on the bottom of the steps, and Thea heard another voice at the top. The man at the bottom turned and walked up a few steps. They stood talking, although Thea couldn't see the man at the top of the stairs. She couldn't see the other man's face, either, but she thought it must be John. Or was it the man she and Nikki had seen the other night who looked like John?

Trapped for the moment, she glanced around the unfamiliar room, realizing almost at once that she was inside Morris Dalrimple's apartment. The furnishings were fussy for a bachelor, even one as peculiar as Dalrimple.

White lace curtains hung at the windows, matching the starched doilies that decorated tabletops and the backs of green velvet chairs. Pictures in heavy ornate frames and lamps with fringed shades gave the room a strangely oppressive air that made Thea shiver.

A wheelchair sat near the hallway, and she realized that even if Morris Dalrimple wasn't home, his mother surely was. How would she explain her presence here?

She glanced through the crack in the door. The two men were still out there talking, arguing it sounded like. Thea was almost convinced now that the one near the bottom of the stairs wasn't John, but she wasn't sure enough to risk being seen by him.

Silently she closed the door and turned to walk slowly into the apartment. "Mrs. Dalrimple?" she called softly, crossing the room to the window. Maybe if she alerted the old lady to her presence, she could make up some excuse for being there and wait until the coast was clear to leave. Then she could go upstairs, get her money and papers, the suitcase she'd left packed for just such an emergency—

Somewhere in the apartment, a floorboard squeaked, and Thea whirled. Gathering her courage, she walked to the tiny hallway and called out again. Still no answer. One of the bedroom doors was open, but she couldn't see anyone inside. The other door was closed, and if the old woman was sleeping, Thea didn't want to awaken her.

Maybe she'd remain asleep until Thea could leave. But what if Morris Dalrimple came home in the meantime? Thea shuddered. She'd say she had come to have tea or something. Or to ask his advice about dealing with the police. The little man would love it, she was sure.

Suppressing another shudder, Thea glanced around the room. It suddenly occurred to her that if Dalrimple had somehow found proof of her and Nikki's real identities, the evidence might be right here in his apartment. And this might be an ideal time to look for it.

Crossing the floor as quietly as she could, Thea began to search through table drawers and baroque boxes filled with papers and mementos. She became so engrossed in her quest that she forgot to listen for footsteps. For the squeak of a door. For the soft *swoosh* of the wheelchair.

The old woman was almost upon her before Thea heard the sound of her raspy breathing.

Chapter Eleven

Morris Dalrimple sat in the wheelchair, a shawl draped over his shoulders. Images of *Psycho* raced through Thea's head. Then Dalrimple laughed, got up from the wheelchair and tossed the shawl aside.

"Had you fooled for a moment, admit it."

He didn't seem at all concerned to have found Thea in his apartment going through his things. She glanced behind him, toward the bedrooms. "Where is your mother?"

"Resting, poor thing. She doesn't have the strength she once did."

If Thea called out, would the old woman hear her? Would she be able to help her?

Did she even exist?

Thea drew a long shaky breath. She had to get out of here. "You must be wondering what I'm doing in your apartment."

"Not at all," Dalrimple said happily. "You've come for tea." He beamed at her almost giddily before turning toward the kitchen.

Something was different about him, Thea noted. He wasn't stumbling over his words. He seemed supremely confident all of a sudden.

"I came in here because I didn't want to be seen by the police," she explained truthfully. "You said yourself I have to be careful."

"So I did." He busied himself with the kettle. Thea edged toward the front door, but stopped when he glanced at her sharply. "He's still out there. If you leave now you'll run smack into Detective Gallagher. You don't want that."

No, she didn't want that, but she didn't want to remain in this apartment with a strange and, for all she knew, very sick little man. "He's probably gone by now. Maybe I should just have a look."

"Thea." Dalrimple's tone held a warning that made her mouth go instantly dry. "You don't want to leave without this, do you?" He came out of the kitchen holding a folded piece of paper in the palm of his hand.

Thea said doubtfully, "What is it?"

He unfolded the paper and held it up for her inspection. Thea's heart crashed against her chest. Somehow he'd found Nikki's birth certificate. He knew who they were. What Thea had done.

She began shaking all over, but managed to say coolly, "You went into my apartment and searched through my things." The image made her almost physically ill. "That's illegal."

Mr. Dalrimple smiled. "Now if that isn't the pot calling the kettle black. What were you doing just now, Thea?"

"That was different. I was looking for whatever you'd taken from me."

"But you didn't know I'd taken anything. This is just a copy. The original is still safe and sound where you left it."

And she thought she'd been so clever. Who would

have thought of taking the plate off an electrical outlet and looking inside? Obviously Dalrimple had. And if he'd found the birth certificate, what else might he have found?

Now her heart plummeted. Had he found her money, the IDs? Had he taken those, too?

"You're the one who called Gail Waters, aren't you?" she said coldly. "She came to see you the night she died. You let her in."

"She wasn't supposed to die," he said sadly.

Fear balled in Thea's stomach. "Then you—"

His expression turned horrified. "I didn't push her. I would never do that! I only wanted to see her that night to try and talk her out of doing a story on you. Mama and I were big fans of hers, you see. We never missed her program. She was so wonderful and so clever! When I found Nicolette's, er, Nikki's birth certificate, I thought it would be something that would, er, interest Gail." Dalrimple gave her an apologetic smile. "But after I'd gotten to, er, know you, I was sorry I'd, er, tipped her off."

Thea wondered if it was a good or bad sign that his halted speech had returned. "What did she say to you that night?"

Dalrimple shrugged. "She said for me not to worry because she was, er, working on a bigger story, anyway, and that she might not be able to use the information she'd found out about you."

Was that the reason Thea hadn't been able to locate a file on her and Nikki in Gail's office? Because they weren't a big enough story?

"What kind of story was she working on?"

Dalrimple shrugged again. "She didn't say, but I have a feeling it involved, er, someone else in the building. I'd seen her come and go a few times from here. That's how I managed to, er, meet her.''

''You don't know who she was coming to see?''

Dalrimple hesitated. His eyes gleamed strangely. ''She was coming to see your baby-sitter.''

Thea stared at him in shock. ''Mrs. Lewellyn?''

''No, no. Bliss Kyler. I saw Gail coming out of her apartment one day.''

''Bliss? But why?'' Thea said it almost to herself, not expecting an answer. If Bliss was somehow connected to Gail Waters, and Bliss was the one who had taken Nikki up to the roof that day...

Thea's head spun in confusion.

From somewhere back in the apartment, a bell tinkled faintly.

Dalrimple looked instantly alarmed. ''That's Mama,'' he said. ''She'll be wanting her, er, tea, and I haven't even heated the, er, water.''

So there really was a Mrs. Dalrimple. Somehow that fact slightly alleviated Thea's uneasiness, although she couldn't say why exactly. She had no reason in the world to believe a word Morris Dalrimple had told her, but in some strange way, it all made sense. He'd found Nikki's birth certificate, realized she and Thea were using aliases and had approached Gail Waters with the information, probably to impress her.

The bell tinkled again, and Dalrimple bustled about the kitchen, readying the tea. ''Coming, Mama!'' To Thea he said, ''You'd better go now. Mama can be a little, er, cranky when she first wakes up.''

He loaded the tray and headed for the bedroom. Thea grabbed the copy of the birth certificate and headed for the door.

Dalrimple paused in the hallway, turning to Thea. A

large yellow tabby rubbed against his leg, and a bell on the cat's collar tinkled when it moved.

A chill snaked up Thea's backbone as her gaze fell on the cat.

Dalrimple gave her an enigmatic smile ''You'll have to come back and meet Mama sometime, Thea. I'm told I look exactly like her.''

THE COAST WAS CLEAR when Thea let herself out of Morris Dalrimple's apartment. She felt as if she'd just escaped from a carnival fun house, but she wouldn't let herself dwell on the condition of Morris Dalrimple's psyche. Instead, she had to get upstairs, get the money and the papers and the suitcase…

Her thoughts trailed away as she started down the hallway toward the stairs. She could see beyond the steps to the glass front door, and beyond that to the street outside. A familiar gray sedan was parked at the curb. It was John's car.

If it had been him she'd seen earlier on the stairs, then he'd either come back or had never left. Now he was somewhere inside the building. She suspected he was in her apartment, looking for more evidence against her.

And if Dalrimple had found the birth certificate, what might a trained police detective be able to find?

JOHN RANG THE BELL and then knocked on Bliss Kyler's door. He'd spoken with her on the phone a day or so ago, but he'd yet to meet her in person. If he didn't know better, he'd think Thea's baby-sitter was avoiding him; he wanted to know why, particularly in light of recent events. Bliss lived only two doors down from Thea. It wasn't beyond the realm of possibility she might have seen or heard something early this morning when someone had tried to break into Thea's apartment.

John turned and surveyed the hallway as he waited for Bliss to answer the bell. When the door was finally opened, a man said angrily, "What are you doing back here? I told you I wouldn't say anything—"

The man stopped abruptly when John turned to face him. His face beneath the goatee and long hair turned pale, but his eyes glittered dangerously.

John said incredulously, "Eddie?"

Eddie Dawson gave him a contemptuous look. "How did you find me?"

"Dumb luck actually," John admitted. He stepped into the apartment before Eddie could close the door on him. "I take it you were expecting someone else."

"What do you want?"

"I'm getting the feeling you're not too happy to see me, Eddie." John strode into the apartment and gazed around. "Nice place you've got here."

Without comment Eddie walked over and picked up a beer bottle from the coffee table and downed the remainder of the contents.

"So who were you expecting?" John asked casually.

"None of your damned business." Eddie sank down in a chair and folded his arms over his bare chest. He glared up at John through bleary bloodshot eyes.

"I'm guessing it was my cousin, Miles."

Something that might have been alarm flickered in Eddie's eyes before he quickly shuttered his expression. "So what if it was? He happens to be a friend of mine."

"A friend with a faulty memory, right?" John sat down facing him on the shabby sofa.

Eddie spread his hands in supplication. "Look, Miles and I have a business relationship, okay? I've got a few connections on the street. I give him a few names once in a while and he gives me a few bucks. No big deal."

John wondered what Superintendent Dawson would do if he found out one of his narcs was using his own son as an informant. There was nothing more dangerous, nothing drug dealers hated more than a fink. Eddie Dawson didn't look particularly brave, but he did look strung out. And a desperate addict would do desperate things.

"Funny," John said. "Both Miles and my brother Tony swore seven years ago that they saw you at that party the night Ashley was murdered, but now it seems Miles isn't so sure. I can't help wondering what made him have a change of heart."

Eddie said bitterly, "I know what you're implying, but I didn't have anything to do with Ashley's death. She was my sister, for God's sake."

"Stepsister."

"So what? That didn't matter to her," he said with a haunted look in his eyes. "She treated me more like family than…" He glanced away.

"Than who? Your father?"

Eddie dragged his fingers through his long tangled hair. "Look, that's all water under the bridge. Ancient history. My old man and I have come to an understanding. He lives his life and I live mine."

"So how did Gail Waters come into the picture?"

"Who says she did?" Eddie's gaze narrowed. "I know you don't have anything. You'd have been here a lot sooner if you did."

"I wasn't here sooner because you're a hard man to

track down," John told him. He sat forward, resting his forearms on his knees. "And I just might know a little more than you think I do. For instance, I've been told you were the one Gail Waters came here to see the night she died. You let her into the building. You may have been the last one to see her alive."

"So prove it." Eddie glared at him, his eyes cold and dangerous.

John smiled. "I also know she didn't come here to talk to you about Ashley's murder or my father's disappearance, although that's what both your father and your stepmother would have me believe. Gail had something a little more personal on her mind, didn't she?"

Eddie snorted with disgust. "I don't know what the hell you're talking about, man."

"You asked her to meet you here, didn't you?"

"Why would I do that?"

John sat back and watched him. "Maybe to try and persuade her to break it off with your father. You and Annette were always pretty tight, weren't you? Maybe you didn't like seeing her hurt. Or maybe—" John paused "—maybe you were trying your hand at blackmail. A little cash always comes in handy, doesn't it, Eddie? Especially when you're needy. Were you helping Gail blackmail your own father?"

Eddie sprang to his feet so fast John was instantly alarmed. He eased his jacket open, ready to reach for his weapon.

But Eddie just stood glaring down at him, his red-rimmed eyes flashing in barely suppressed rage. "Does he know you're here?"

"Who? The superintendent?" Very slowly John rose to his feet, taking away Eddie's advantage.

"You don't know what kind of trouble you're walking into, man. You don't know."

"Why don't you tell me?"

Eddie just shook his head. "No one crosses him. I mean, no one. Look at me. I'm living proof."

John gave him a long hard appraisal. "You blame your father for the way your life's turned out? Come on, Eddie. You're a big boy."

The criticism didn't seem to register. Or maybe he just didn't care. He scratched a tattoo on his left arm. "The only decent thing he ever did was marry Annette. And then he had to go and mess that up, too."

"With Gail? Is that why he and your stepmother split up?"

Eddie shrugged. "Annette should have left him years ago if you ask me, but she didn't. For some reason she still loves him. I thought if I could give Gail Waters what she wanted, she'd back off. Give them a chance to reconcile."

"What did Gail want?"

"Information. A story. One big enough to get her some national attention. She wanted to be the next Barbara Walters." Eddie laughed, a harsh grating sound. "Pretty funny when you think about it. A young beautiful reporter pursuing Super Cop, feeding his middle-age ego, breaking up his marriage, and all for the sake of pillow talk."

"You mean she started the affair just so she could get information from your father?"

"They say men are the stronger sex, but women have all the power," Eddie said bitterly. "Especially the good-looking ones."

John thought unaccountably of Thea. She was undeniably beautiful and she did have power over him.

He wanted to believe she was unaware of that power, but he couldn't be sure she wasn't *using* his attraction to her for some reason. Why else had he not gone to her and demanded an explanation about her voice on the 911 tape? Or the button he'd found in Gail Waters's office?

Why else was he busting his ass, trying to find other suspects in the Waters case?

"Did you see Gail the night she died?" John asked him.

Eddie shook his head. "I buzzed her in, but she never showed up at the door."

"You didn't go looking for her? You didn't wonder what had happened to her? The time it would take for her to enter the front door, climb the stairs and knock on your door couldn't be more than two minutes, tops. You didn't think it strange when she didn't show up?"

"I figured she changed her mind, got cold feet. Then the next day I heard on TV she'd jumped off the roof, for God's sake."

"And you never considered coming forward and sharing this information? You used to be a cop, Eddie."

"Yeah, used to be." He shrugged. "Anyway, I'm giving you the information now....*Johnny.*"

And the question was, why now? What was Eddie's angle? Was he deliberately trying to make his father look guilty out of revenge? Or because he was trying to protect someone else? Annette? Himself?

"Why was Miles really coming to see you, Eddie?"

The question seemed to startle him. His bloodshot eyes widened. "I told you, man. We have a business arrangement."

"He gives you money for the names of a few penny-ante pushers. What did you give him for forgetting you were at that frat party seven years ago?''

Eddie licked his lips. ''You're on the wrong track. Gail's death had nothing to do with seven years ago.''

''What do you have on Miles?''

''Nothing. It's not *like* that.''

''Did Miles know Gail, too? Is that it?'' It was a stab in the dark, but John thought he might have hit pay dirt. If Liam suspected his own son was somehow involved, what better reason for him to be so resistant to John's investigation? What better way to call John off than to warn him his own brother could become a suspect if he pursued the case? Was Tony really the one Liam was so worried about?

Was John really so desperate to clear Thea that he was willing to think the worst of his own family?

He knew nothing about the woman. She was almost a complete stranger to him. If she was so innocent, why had she been in Gail Waters's office last night? Why had she tried to hide her connection to the dead woman? What did Gail Waters have on her?

Someone close to him could be a cold-blooded murderer, John thought, as he left Eddie's apartment. Miles. Liam. Eddie Dawson and his stepmother. Superintendent Dawson—the Super Cop, as Eddie had called him.

The list was almost overwhelming, but the most daunting name of all was Thea's. She could be the killer, and for all John knew, Gail Waters hadn't even been her first victim.

JOHN GOT HOME just after seven that night, and he brought Chinese takeout. Thea's stomach had been in knots all day, while she waited for him to get back.

Because she'd suspected he'd been in her apartment, she hadn't risked going in to retrieve her money or the IDs, and without either of those, she and Nikki would not last long on the streets. Too many people, including John, would be looking for them.

She set the table as he unloaded the food from the bags, and as she reached over to place a napkin near one of the plates, her hand brushed his. A thrill of awareness shot through her, and when she glanced up, she found his gaze, dark and intense, on her.

Thea shivered, wondering what he was thinking. How much he knew. Should she just confess and get it over with?

Don't do it, a little voice warned her. *He'll turn you in.*

What else could she expect? He was a cop, an officer of the law. He'd have to do the right thing.

But there were extenuating circumstances. Would he understand that?

"Smells good," she said, straightening from the table and backing away a little.

"So," John asked, "what have you been doing all day?"

"Trying to keep Nikki occupied." She paused. "Your sister dropped by and brought her some toys. That was very thoughtful."

"Fiona has her moments."

"Actually she stayed with Nikki for a while so that I could run some errands."

"What kind of errands?"

Thea shrugged. "Nothing special. Nikki and I just needed some things. I really have to get back into my apartment, John."

He nodded. "How about tomorrow? That soon enough?"

It would have to be. Thea swallowed. "Yes. That'll be fine."

"If you're planning on going back to work, you'll need your uniforms, won't you?"

The question sounded innocent, but Thea's heart immediately began to pound. She started to turn away, but his hand snaked out and grasped her shoulder.

"Don't do that, Thea."

"What?" She shivered beneath his touch.

"Don't turn away. No more evasions. Just tell me the truth. Were you in Gail Waters's office last night?"

She closed her eyes briefly. "Please don't ask me that."

"Dammit—"

She put her hand on his chest, as if to hold him at bay, but in fact, he hadn't moved any closer. "Don't ask any more questions, John. Just let Nikki and me walk out that door. You'll never hear from us again."

He looked at her incredulously. "Are you out of your mind? Where would you go? How would you live?"

"That's none of your concern."

"The hell it's not. Someone tried to break into your apartment last night, Thea. You and Nikki could have been killed. How long do you think the two of you would last on the streets?"

She'd asked herself that same question not more than five minutes ago, but somehow hearing it from him made the prospect seem even more dismal. She had to take care of Nikki, protect her at all costs, but she couldn't do that out on the streets. She couldn't do it here, with John, either. She'd never felt so trapped in her life.

His other hand came up to grasp her other shoulder, and he held her at arm's length before slowly beginning to pull her toward him. "You have to level with me here. I can't help you if you don't."

"If I tell you the truth, you won't be able to help me," she whispered.

"So what am I supposed to do? Close my eyes? Let you and Nikki walk away?" He drew her toward him, inch by torturous inch. "I can't do that."

Thea was suddenly in his arms, and his head lowered swiftly to hers. The kiss was neither gentle nor punishing. It was, quite simply, devastating. Thea's eyes fluttered closed as she trembled in his arms, and she parted her lips, responding to his urgency. This was the last thing in the world she needed, and yet she couldn't stop it. Didn't *want* to stop it.

John was everything she'd ever wanted in a man, she realized with an insight that took her breath away. He was strong and caring, confident enough in his own masculinity to admit to his weaknesses, to let her glimpse beyond his badge and gun to the loneliness and longing that matched her own.

He kissed her as if he would never let her go, and when his arms came around her waist, drawing her even closer, she reveled in his strength. Her hands moved to his chest, but she was no longer trying to hold him at bay. Instead, she flattened a palm over his heart, letting the beat match the wild rhythm of hers.

He broke the kiss to nuzzle her neck, then to whisper heatedly against her ear, "Don't ask me to let you walk away."

"You don't know me," she whispered back, despite

the shiver raging up her backbone. ''You don't know anything about me.''

He drew back to gaze down into her upturned face. His eyes were like blue flames, hot, burning. The eyes of a man deeply aroused. ''Then tell me.''

''I...can't.''

''Thea—''

She backed out of his arms, feeling a chill descend over her heart. ''Don't ask questions you don't really want the answers to.'' She turned at that and walked out of the room without looking back.

DINNER WAS AWKWARD. Thea wasn't the least bit hungry, but she tried to pretend an appetite for Nikki's sake. Her daughter was very sensitive to the moods around her, and Thea didn't want her own anxiety to affect Nikki. She needed to eat and keep up her strength, because the coming days and nights were likely to be trying for both of them.

John barely said two words all through the meal, and afterward, he insisted on cleaning up while Thea gave Nikki her bath. She tucked her daughter into bed and tarried so long over a story that Nikki was sound asleep long before Thea put down the book.

She kissed her daughter's cheek and then crossed the room on tiptoe, leaving the door ajar so she could hear if Nikki became restless during the night.

There was nothing to do but go out into the living room and face John. Their earlier conversation—not to mention the kiss—had lingered all through dinner until the tension between them had become almost unbearable. And it was still there, in the way Thea reluctantly entered the room, in the way John's gaze seemed to track her every move.

He'd been sitting in the recliner by the fire, his head back, an arm thrown over his eyes when she'd first come in. She'd thought for a moment he was asleep, but then his arm slid away, and she knew he'd been watching her the whole time.

She shivered, putting her hands out toward the fire. "I've been thinking."

John didn't say anything, but she heard the leather chair squeak as he got up. She could feel his presence behind her, but she didn't turn. With the same will that had kept her sane the past four months, she forced herself not to react to his proximity.

"It would be better for all of us if Nikki and I left here. Not tonight," she said hurriedly. "I have to…pick up some things from the apartment. But tomorrow morning. As soon as possible."

"As simple as that."

She turned then and found that he was closer than she'd thought. He was very tall, and he seemed almost overpowering to her at that moment. "It's not simple," she said with a sigh. "Nothing about this is simple."

"You've got that right," he agreed.

"But it is the only way."

He folded his arms and stared down at her. Firelight danced in his eyes, but the heat she saw now was a mirage. There was no longer passion in those blue depths, only suspicion. "I found a button from one of your uniforms in Gail Waters's office last night, not to mention the fact that your voice was on the 911 tape."

Thea closed her eyes briefly. She'd tried to disguise her voice, and had it not been for the button, she was fairly certain she could have pulled it off.

He reached out as if to hold her, then changed his mind and dropped his arms to his side. "Considering all that, I'm just supposed to stand aside and let you walk away without asking any questions? Do you know what you're asking of me?''

Thea swallowed. "Yes. I do.''

"I don't think so. I don't think you have any idea. I'm a cop, for God's sake, and the moment you went into that office last night, you became a suspect. Do you understand that?''

Her hand crept to her throat in fear. "Are you saying you're going to arrest me?''

He gave her a withering look. "I'm saying I want some answers. What the hell were you doing in Waters's office last night?''

"I didn't kill her, John. I didn't have anything to do with her death. That Nikki and I got involved at all was just a bizarre coincidence.''

"And your being in her office last night—that was a coincidence, too?'' His voice had turned sarcastic, and Thea flinched.

"I can't tell you why I went there. If I told you—''

"You'd have to kill me, right?''

"That's not funny,'' Thea said angrily. "You don't understand. I have to think of Nikki.''

"And you think I'm not?'' He stared at the fire. "Why won't you let me help you?''

"Because you can't. No one can. Please…''

John didn't think he'd ever heard anyone sound so hopeless, so beseeching. Thea was a proud woman. She wouldn't beg for herself, but she would do anything for her daughter. That was one of the things that made her so appealing.

He'd tried to stay away from her, tried to keep his hands off her, but he couldn't help himself now. He turned to her, trailing the back of his hand down the side of her face. She closed her eyes, trembling.

"What have you done?" he asked her softly.

She drew a long quivering breath. "I didn't kill Gail Waters," she said again. "If Nikki and I left, it wouldn't affect your investigation at all. We don't know anything. Nikki didn't see anything."

"But what if the killer thinks otherwise? Are you willing to take that chance, Thea?"

"I may not have a choice."

"We all have choices," John said grimly. "We just may not like the ones we have."

Chapter Twelve

John insisted that Thea take his bedroom. She'd put up a token argument, but the truth was, she was glad for the privacy. She needed to be alone to sort through her feelings, weigh her options, decide what she should do.

But when she went into the bedroom and found her purse and suitcase lying on John's bed, the seriousness of her situation hit her again. John had been in her apartment today. He'd taken her suitcase. Had he also found the money? Her papers? Had Morris Dalrimple told him about Nikki's birth certificate?

Suddenly the guilt and fear of the past four months came crashing down on her, and she felt as if she was smothering. She wanted to tell John the truth. She *needed* to tell him, but there was danger in that need. If she told him what she'd done, he'd have to make a choice—turn her in or help her escape. Was it fair to put that burden on him?

But if he found out on his own—and he was bound to sooner or later—he would hear the Mancusos' version and the police's. He wouldn't know about the extenuating circumstances, the four years of stalking and threats, the constant terror.

All John would know was that she had killed someone. Another cop. And if she'd murdered once, why couldn't she have done it again? Why shouldn't John believe that a woman who had shot her ex-husband in cold blood had also gone up to the roof that night and pushed a reporter who knew too much to her death?

Maybe it was better that he hear it from her. Maybe the truth was her only way out now.

Shoving the hair from her face, Thea went back out to the living room. John was lying on the sofa, his arms folded behind his head as he gazed into the fire. He turned his head toward her the moment she walked into the room.

"I need to tell you what happened," she said quietly.

He wore dark blue sweatpants and nothing else. Thea could see the ripple of muscle in his arms and shoulders as he tossed the blanket aside.

He said nothing, and after a moment Thea gathered her courage and crossed the room to the sofa. He took her arm and pulled her down beside him. There was strength in his touch. Comfort. Thea resisted the urge to lay her head on his shoulder, to let the world fade away in his arms. But that wasn't meant to be. That couldn't be.

"My father was murdered five years ago," she began. "Other than my stepmother, he was the only family I had. We were very close. His death did something to me. I think I went off the deep end for a little while. All I could think about was getting justice for him. Making sure his killer got what he deserved."

John said nothing. He sat quietly listening to her, his blue eyes unfathomable in the firelight.

"The homicide detective in charge of the investigation was young and very…intense." Thea shivered, remembering. "He worked on the case tirelessly, night and day, seven days a week. He became almost as obsessed with finding the killer as I was. I guess that obsession somehow drew us together, bonded us..."

"It happens," John said softly.

Thea shrugged. "It took months, but he never gave up, and when he finally made the arrest, it was like...I don't know how to explain it. It was like I owed him something. I convinced myself I was in love with him, and we got married before we ever really got to know each other.

"He came from a big family. A family of cops." She paused, glancing at John. A frown flickered across his forehead. She suspected he was remembering a conversation they'd had days ago. Days? It seemed like years. "They were...very close. I didn't realize how close until one of his brothers was brought up on charges of police brutality. He was accused of beating a teenage boy to death after a concert one night. The whole family just went berserk. They were like...wild animals, protecting their pack. I'd never seen anything like it." She shuddered. "When the charges were dropped a few days later, I always suspected they'd done something to the boy's family, threatened them somehow."

"What did you do?" John asked her.

"I left him. I couldn't deal with all that anger, that violence. We'd only been married a few months, but I'd known almost from the start that it had been a mistake. When I moved out he...reacted badly. At first he begged me to come back. He sent me flowers, candy, everything. Then he became angry. He started threatening me."

John muttered a curse under his breath. Thea had never heard him use such a word.

"It might have all blown over if he hadn't found out I was pregnant. Then his mother started coming to see me. She was...unreasonable. She threatened to take my baby away from me if I didn't reconcile with her son. But there was no way, by this time, that I was going to go back. I knew I'd have to fight them for custody, but I never dreamed the extent to which they'd go."

A muscle worked in John's cheek. "What did they do?"

"He always had someone following me, one of his brothers or one of his friends on the force. They harassed me continually, slit my tires, made obscene phone calls in the middle of the night. But the worst happened at the custody hearing. He got his brothers and friends to swear they'd...been with me. That I had come on to them. And his mother told the jury I was an unfit mother, that I neglected Nikki and...worse. I almost lost my daughter, and I couldn't stand the thought of that family raising her."

John still wasn't touching her, but Thea could feel the warmth of his gaze, the heat of his anger—not at her, but at a man he'd never met. Would never meet.

"So that's it," he said. "You lost custody of Nikki, so you kidnapped her. You've been on the run with her ever since."

Thea closed her eyes briefly. "No, I got custody."

She stood up to move over by the fire, letting the warmth penetrate her chill for a moment before she turned back to face John. "I got custody, but my ex-husband got visitation rights. I couldn't leave the state. Every other weekend, Nikki had to go stay with him and his family, and she always came back...different. It's difficult to explain, but she has always been a very sensitive child. She feels things deeply. That's one of the things that makes her so special, but her father despised her sensitivity.

"He berated her, tried to make her do things she didn't want to do—like forcing her down a slide that terrified her." Thea paused. "I dreaded those weekends. It tore me apart, watching her go off with him, knowing that every time she came back, a part of her was always missing..."

John rose and went to stand beside her. He took her in his arms and held her close, smoothing his hand down her hair. "I wish I'd been there," he said, and the coldness in his voice, the latent quiver of rage made Thea tremble.

She pushed herself away from him. "That went on for two years. And when he didn't have Nikki, he and his family continued to terrorize me, stalking me, threatening me. The phone calls continued. It was like living in hell, but there was nothing I could do legally. I couldn't prove anything. And I'd already seen how they would lie for one another in court, what they would do to someone who threatened them."

Her hand shook as she reached up to tuck a strand of hair behind her ear. "His...obsession with me just kept getting stronger. I was terrified he'd do something to me, and then he would get Nikki. I couldn't stand the thought of her being with him, being raised by that family..." She paused again, taking a deep breath. "I knew there might come a time when I would have to take Nikki away to protect her. I began making preparations, keeping a packed suitcase ready and a lot of cash on hand. I even had one of my father's associates get us sets of false IDs and papers. I was prepared for the worst."

"What happened?" John asked.

''He broke into our house one night. He was drunk, out of control, and he started hitting me. I tried to fight back, but he was too strong. When he thought he'd knocked me out, he started for Nikki's room. That's when I lost control. I kept a gun my father had given me years ago locked in my nightstand drawer. I got the gun and I shot him.''

John was totally silent. When the fire crackled, Thea jumped. She rubbed her hands up and down her arms, but the chill that had come over her wouldn't be abated now. Whether John believed her or not, she didn't know, and at the moment, she was too drained to even care.

''I killed him,'' she said numbly. ''There was blood everywhere. Nikki came running in and saw him lying there. Saw the gun in my hand...'' Thea dropped her head. ''I'll never forget her scream that night. She hasn't uttered a word since.''

And with that, Thea turned and walked out of the room, leaving John's awful silence behind her.

A HOT SHOWER did little to relax her. Or to warm her. Thea huddled beneath the covers in John's bed, agonizing over whether she'd done the right thing. She hadn't mentioned any names. By the time John was able to figure out the rest, she and Nikki could be long gone.

But the thought of running for the rest of her life, never having a real home for her daughter, never having anyone to share their lives with. Never again knowing love...

The bedroom door was open, and light from the hallway spilled in. Thea's heart started to pound when John moved into the room to stand at the foot of the bed.

He said nothing for the longest moment, just stood looking at her. His eyes in the dim light looked fierce, almost savage.

"If you hadn't killed him, I would have."

She almost didn't recognize his voice. The darkness in his tone should have frightened her but somehow didn't. Slowly he moved around to the side of the bed. "I don't want you and Nikki to leave here tomorrow. I want you to stay. I want you to let me help you—"

"John—"

"Don't say it." He sat down on the edge of the bed, not touching her, but making her ache for his touch. "You can't do this alone, Thea. Not anymore. You have to trust me."

"I don't know if I can. What happens if someone else finds out about me? What happens to your career?"

"To hell with that."

"That's what you say now, but what about tomorrow? Next week? Next year? I won't let you sacrifice everything for us."

"I don't think I have a choice," he said quietly. He stroked a finger down her arm, and Thea trembled, closing her eyes.

"You said we all have choices. We may not like the ones we have."

"I was wrong. I don't think either of us has a choice. Thea, look at me."

She did, then glanced away before she could see the longing, passion smoldering in his eyes. She wanted him, too, but this couldn't happen. It would make it all that much harder to leave.

He put his knuckles under her chin and turned her to him. The moment their gazes met, Thea's heart started to race. He was only inches away, touching her with his eyes and not his hands. As if mesmerized, Thea rose to her knees before him, threading her hands through his hair, bending to kiss him with an intensity she never knew she possessed.

His arms were instantly around her, drawing her across his lap, twisting her so that her breasts were crushed to his chest. The kiss was overwhelming, the emotions between them so powerful Thea was completely breathless when he broke away. He rose long enough to close the bedroom door, and then he was back, reaching for her again, pressing her back against the pillows as he joined their mouths once more.

He ripped at the buttons on her pajamas, she tore at his pants. The clothes scattered until there was nothing between them but the heat of their passion, the warmth of their need.

"Don't worry," he whispered against her ear when a flash of reality might have intruded. "I'll protect you. I'll take care of everything," he murmured, reaching for the nightstand drawer.

WHEN IT WAS OVER, he rolled onto his back and they lay side by side, staring at the ceiling. Thea's heart still pounded, but second thoughts had almost immediately began to assail her. What had she done?

Beside her, John's breathing was as ragged as her own. "Don't have regrets," he said as if reading her mind.

"It's difficult not to." She started to get up, but he reached over and grasped her hand, pulling her back down to him.

Very gently he smoothed the dark curls from her

forehead. "I meant what I said, Thea. I'll protect you. I'll take care of everything."

She closed her eyes against a wave of terrible yearning. If only he could.

THEA AWAKENED from a dream with the sound of Nikki's sweet voice lingering in her ears. "Mommy! Mommy!"

Thea bolted upright in bed. It wasn't a dream! Nikki was calling her. She bounded out of bed, grabbing for her robe.

John was awake, too, and reaching for his pants, but Thea said quickly, "No, I'll go."

She raced down the hallway to Nikki's room, throwing the door wide open. She wasn't sure what she'd expected, but Nikki was sitting up in bed, rubbing her eyes with her fists.

Thea hurried over to the bed and sat down on the edge. "What is it, sweetheart? Did you have a bad dream?"

Nikki pulled away from Thea, then lay back down and snuggled beneath the covers. Within moments she was sound asleep again.

Thea sat with her for a long time, but then, when she was sure Nikki wouldn't awaken again, she got up and tiptoed from the room.

John was standing in the hallway, and Thea knew he'd been watching her and Nikki from the doorway. She found she didn't mind.

She leaned against the wall, a flood of emotions rushing through her. "She called out to me, John. My baby called me."

"I heard her," he said gruffly, and then he pulled Thea into his arms, letting her weep against his chest.

When John got to the station the next morning, Roy Cox informed him that his uncle had been looking for him earlier. "He's on the warpath," Roy warned.

John grimaced. Evidently his visit to Annette Dawson yesterday had already been reported, and now it was time to face the music. Which was fine, he thought grimly. He had a few questions for his uncle, as well.

Liam's office door was closed, and through the frosted-glass window, John could see that his uncle had at least two visitors. The first thing he thought was that they were from Internal Affairs. Someone—Mrs. Dawson or even the superintendent—had lodged a formal complaint against him, which meant his investigation would be halted while he, himself, was investigated.

He started to back away from the door when everyone inside rose. Whoever was in there was about to leave, and John decided he'd just hang around for a few minutes, see who came out. He backed down the corridor, keeping out of sight in the watercooler niche.

The door to Liam's office opened, and John heard voices—his uncle's, another man's and one that sounded like his mother.

He glanced up from the watercooler to see Maggie Gallagher and Superintendent Dawson standing in the corridor outside Liam's office. Liam stood in the doorway, and the three of them spoke in low urgent tones. Then Liam went back inside and closed the door, leaving John's mother and Dawson alone in the hallway. She put her hand on the man's sleeve as she spoke to him again, and then Dawson turned and headed toward the exit.

Maggie Gallagher started down the hallway in John's direction. When John stepped out of the alcove, she saw him, and her hand flew to her heart. "Johnny! I…was just coming to see you."

He lifted a brow. "What brings you down here?" She hadn't been to the station in years, and there was something a little troubling about her presence, about her meeting with Liam and the superintendent, about the way she'd touched Dawson's arm.

The word "intimate" sprang to John's mind, but he tried to dismiss it. His mother had never even looked at another man since his father's disappearance. Besides which, Ed Dawson was still a married man, and his wife was Maggie's friend.

She looked different today, John noticed with a frown. The dark green tailored suit she wore made her look younger and slimmer, and she had on makeup, too, a subtle color on her eyelids and a vivid red on her lips. John had never seen his mother look this way before.

She took his arm and started walking down the hall toward his office. "I was just talking to Liam and Ed about Mac's retirement party tonight. You haven't forgotten, have you?"

"Uh, no," John said, but of course he had. He'd had a lot on his mind lately, not the least of which was the night he'd just spent with Thea.

He'd never known a woman like her before, never thought to feel this way again. Maybe he'd never felt this way.

"Have you seen your brothers lately?" his mother asked.

"I saw Tony a couple of weeks ago." He'd looked like hell, too, but John didn't think he'd pass that detail along to their mother. "I've been trying to get in touch with him the last day or so, but he's playing hard to get."

"That sounds like Tony." She smiled, but her eyes looked worried. "Johnny...you're not going to ask him about Ashley, are you? You're not going to drag all that up now, are you?"

"You've been talking to Liam about more than just a retirement party," John said dryly. So they'd enlisted his own mother against him. What the hell were they all trying to cover up?

His mother sighed. "I know you can't walk away from an investigation, no matter who might get hurt. You're so much like your father..." Her words trailed off and she glanced away. "But Tony doesn't need to be reminded about Ashley's death. He's never gotten over it."

"I know that, Mom. I don't want to hurt Tony. I don't want to hurt anyone. But if someone killed Gail Waters, I can't pick and choose my leads. The truth is, she was investigating Dad's disappearance when she died. And Dad's disappearance and Ashley's murder are irrevocably linked. You can't investigate one without the other. If Gail Waters was murdered because of something she found out—"

His mother's grip tightened on his arm. "You can't really believe that. Ashley's murder was solved, and your father's disappearance—"

"Wasn't." He paused, then said, "Look, for whatever it's worth, I'm not altogether convinced Gail Waters's death had anything to do with seven years ago. That could be a false lead." He wondered if his mother knew or suspected that Ed Dawson had been having an affair with Gail Waters at the time of her death. For some reason John didn't want to be the one to tell her.

They both fell silent for a moment, then his mother glanced over her shoulder, as if concerned they might be overheard. She leaned toward him. "Promise me you'll be careful, Johnny."

He gazed down at her in surprise. "I'm always careful. You know that."

"I know you think you are, but you're not invincible, even though you sometimes feel you have to carry the weight of the world on your shoulders."

John frowned. "Now you sound like Nick."

Her gaze clouded. "You two boys break my heart, you know that, don't you?"

"Sibling rivalry," John said lightly. "Don't take it so seriously."

"I wish that's all it was." She sighed deeply, but then apparently forced herself to brighten. "At least we can all be together tonight. I'm expecting you to be there, Johnny, so don't let me down. Mac will be very disappointed if you don't show."

Mac McCormick had been one of John's father's closest friends. He was throwing in his papers after forty years, and John's mother was giving him the requisite party. "I'll try to make it then."

"Come early and help with the drinks."

Drinks? What had happened to coolers of beer on the patio?

John gazed down at his mother again, this time noticing how shiny her hair looked today. The streaks of gray were missing and the style was different. Maggie Gallagher had undergone a transformation since the last time he'd seen her. What he wanted to know, but wouldn't ask, was why.

When Roy Cox saw them at the door of the office, he swung his legs off his desk and stubbed out his cigar, waving the smoke away with one hand. "Maggie! What brings you down here?"

Maggie? Since when had his mother and his partner been on a first-name basis? They barely knew each other.

"Now, Roy," Maggie said, "you're coming to Mac's party tonight, aren't you?"

"I wouldn't miss it for the world," Roy drawled.

"Oh, good." The two exchanged a smile, a man-woman kind of smile, and John thought, *What the hell...?*

His mother turned back to him, her cheeks tinged an attractive pink, and for the first time since he'd been a kid, John realized how pretty she was. She'd had him when she was eighteen, so that made her fifty-six, still a relatively young woman. And Roy was what? Forty-five, fifty?

With something of a shock John realized his mother was more a contemporary of his partner's than he himself was. But obviously the revelation had occurred to Roy some time ago, and John couldn't help remembering the feminine voice he'd heard in the background when Roy had called night before last.

That hadn't been... No way in hell could that have been...

"What time do you want me, Maggie?" Roy asked her.

She gave a little flip of her wrist. "Oh, around seven. Bring your appetite."

"Yes, ma'am, I surely will."

John smothered an oath.

His mother said, "Well, I'd better be getting home. Fiona's coming over later, and she's taking me to her stylist to get my hair done. We had a makeover together last week, and it was so much fun.'' Her laugh was girlish and breathless, and Roy's awareness was almost palpable. He was practically salivating.

So Fiona was behind this new image. John should have known. He said gruffly, ''I didn't think there was anything wrong with the way you looked before.''

''Oh, you men. What do you know?'' She waggled her fingers at Roy and blew John a kiss. ''See you both later.''

She left the office on a cloud of perfume, and Roy muttered something John didn't catch.

''What?'' John demanded.

''Nothing. I just said it was nice to see your mother again. She's looking…well.''

That wasn't what he'd said, and they both knew it. John scowled at him. ''I need to talk to you about the Gail Waters case.''

''Why? The investigation is being buried, from what I hear. I figured that's what the old man wanted to see you about.''

''Not if I have anything to say about it,'' John snapped.

''You're asking for trouble,'' Roy warned.

''And you can keep your opinions to yourself.''

And while you're at it, keep your slimy hands off my mother.

Chapter Thirteen

John found a parking place at the curb a few houses down from his mother's. He got out and opened the door for Thea and Nikki, and the three of them walked down the sidewalk together. As they approached the stoop, Thea said nervously, "Are you sure it's okay for Nikki and me to be here?"

"It's a big party," John said. "The more the merrier, and besides, how much safer could Nikki be than in a houseful of cops?" He grimaced almost as soon as the words were out of his mouth, as if he recalled too late the story Thea had told him last night. "She'll be fine, Thea. You both will."

Thea wished she could be as certain. Her stomach was in knots, partly in fear, yes, but also because of what had happened between her and John last night. They hadn't spoken about it today, hadn't said much of anything to each other. And they certainly hadn't touched. That would be tempting fate again, she thought, shivering as she remembered the way John had touched her last night. The way he'd kissed her and caressed her...

Her grip tightened on Nikki's hand as John opened the front door and ushered them inside. The living room was large, but the boisterous crowd had spilled into the dining room and kitchen. Fiona saw them immediately and came over to greet them.

After giving John a quick hug and a peck on the cheek, she said, ''Here, let me take your coats.''

She stooped, helping Nikki out of hers while John slipped Thea's off her shoulders. His fingers brushed her neck ever so lightly, and a thrill of awareness shot through her.

''I'm so happy you came,'' Fiona said to Nikki, and then standing, she gave Thea a quick hug. ''I'm glad you came, too.'' She eyed Thea's cranberry-red sweater set and black wool pants—which had been packed in her suitcase—approvingly. ''You look great.''

''Thanks. So do you,'' Thea said, and meant it. Fiona wore an emerald-green sweater and short skirt that showed off her long legs.

She gathered all the coats and said, ''I'll be right back.''

''Let's get something to drink,'' John suggested, and they started through the mass of people.

A woman about Thea's size, with dark hair and gorgeous green eyes, held court in the living room. Women surrounded her, oohing and ahhing over the baby she held in her arms, while a tall blond man hovered protectively over her.

When the woman spotted John, her eyes lit up. ''John! Come over here! You have to meet Christopher.''

Thea sensed John's hesitation, then felt his hand against the small of her back, urging her forward, as if he had no intention of leaving her and Nikki behind.

John nodded to the woman with the baby and the man standing behind her. "Meredith. Vince."

The man nodded back. "John."

They both sounded cordial but strained as the woman proudly exhibited her bald-headed baby for John's inspection. "Isn't he something?"

"Good-looking kid you've got there," John said.

Meredith beamed, and Vince looked a little cocky. He reached over Meredith's shoulder and let the baby grab his finger. Thea wasn't sure what was going on, but she sensed some kind of tension.

Nikki dropped Thea's hand, and glancing down, Thea saw that her daughter had shifted her doll so that she could slip her hand into John's. It was as if she, too, sensed the tension and wanted to make John feel better.

The action wasn't lost on Meredith. She glanced from Nikki to Thea, and her dark brows lifted. "I don't believe we've met."

"This is Thea," John said. "And this is Nikki."

A woman emerged from the crowd with a little squeal of delight. She was perhaps in her fifties, but still very slender and attractive, a mature version of Fiona, but with dark hair.

"What a *darling* little girl!" she cried. She patted John's arm almost absently. "I'm so glad you came, dear. But who have we here?" She knelt and smiled at Nikki.

"This is Nikki," John said, "and her mother, Thea. And this is *my* mother."

"Call me Maggie." She saw the doll Nikki clutched and said admiringly, "And what a pretty thing she is, too. I have a wonderful doll collection upstairs, Nikki.

Everything from baby dolls to Barbie dolls. Would you like to see them?''

Nikki didn't respond, but Maggie rose and took her hand from John's. "Don't worry," she said to Thea. "I'll bring her right back."

She led Nikki away from the crowd, and Thea saw her daughter turn and look back at her. "Maybe I should go with them," she murmured.

"She'll be fine," John said. "Mom's great with kids."

Maybe he was right. Even though Nikki had looked back at her, she didn't seem unduly distressed.

"Come on," John said in Thea's ear. "Let's get that drink."

It was the first time they'd been alone since last night, although, of course, they weren't truly alone. There were dozens of people around, a din of chatter and laughter, but somehow everything faded when John looked at her.

Thea's breath caught in her throat as he took her arm and led her away from the crowd. But rather than going into the kitchen, he pulled her into an alcove beneath the stairs, and before Thea could protest, he bent and kissed her deeply.

Her heart immediately started to pound. She lifted her hand to his chest as his fingertips traced her jawline. When they broke apart, he said, "I've been wanting to do that all day."

Thea realized she'd been wanting that all day, too, even knowing it was dangerous to get so close to him, that nothing could come of it. She gazed up at him, smiling, as she put her finger to his lips. "Lipstick," she whispered.

He pulled out his handkerchief and finished the job.

"I don't know why I'm bothering," he said. "Because I intend to do that again before the night's over."

"Oh, really? What would your mother say if she saw us?" Thea teased.

"About damn time." He grinned. "Or something similar. She's been worried I'd never get married again."

Married? Thea's heart beat even faster. "Was your first marriage so bad?"

He shrugged. "No worse than some. We both made a lot of mistakes." He frowned slightly. "I don't really want to talk about my ex-wife, though. I promised you a drink, didn't I? Wait right here." He started to leave, then turned back quickly, brushing his lips against hers once more. "Don't go anywhere."

"I won't."

Their gazes locked for a moment, and then John turned and headed toward the kitchen. Thea climbed partway up the stairs and sat down. From her vantage, she could watch the party and also wait for Nikki to come back downstairs with John's mother.

The dark-haired woman, minus the baby, sauntered over. "It's Thea, right?" She sat down on the stair below. "I'm Meredith."

"Yes, I remember. Your baby is adorable," Thea said.

The woman's green eyes sparkled. "I think so, too. And your little girl is precious."

"Thank you."

They fell silent, having made the requisite compliments on each other's children. Then Meredith said casually, "How long have you known John?"

"Not long. A few days."

Her dark brows soared. "Really? Only a few days?

Hmm.'' She seemed to contemplate Thea's response. ''Then you probably don't know anyone else here.''

Thea shrugged. ''I'm afraid not.''

''Maybe I can give you a quick lesson.'' Meredith stood and climbed another step so that she could sit next to Thea. ''Okay, see that white-haired man over there next to the window? That's John's uncle Liam. We'll be throwing him one of these bashes in another few years, and the elderly woman beside him—that's Colleen, his mother. John's grandmother. She's a darling.''

There was a striking family resemblance, Thea noted, not so much perhaps in the facial structure but in the eyes. Both Liam and Colleen had the same blue eyes as John.

''Oh, and that man who just came in—the really good-looking one wearing the black leather jacket. That's Nick, John's brother.''

The man Meredith pointed to was, as she said, very good-looking, with hair a shade darker than John's. The strands glinted blue-black in the overhead lighting, but he had the same blue eyes. Also the same tall muscular build.

''What about the man he's talking to?'' Thea asked. ''Is that one of John's brothers, too?''

''No, that's Miles. He's a cousin. Liam's son.''

Thea studied the man for a moment, disturbed for some reason. Then she remembered. He was the man she and Nikki had met on the stairs in their building, the one she'd thought looked so much like John. But why had John's cousin been at the apartment building that night? she wondered uneasily. Was he investigating Gail Waters's death, too?

''The pretty blonde over there in the corner all

lovey-dovey with that cute guy? That's Miles's sister, Kaitlin, and her husband, Dylan O'Roarke.'' Meredith paused, arching Thea a glance. ''You won't know about the O'Roarkes, of course, but—''

''The feud, you mean?''

Meredith glanced at her in surprise. ''Well. I see you've been around a little more than I thought. But yes, there is a feud between the two families. Liam won't allow Kaitlin in his house so long as she's with Dylan O'Roarke, but Maggie's not like that, thank God. She's very...forgiving.'' Something flickered in Meredith's eyes that Thea couldn't define. ''The man next to the fireplace, the distinguished one with the silver hair—that's Superintendent Dawson,'' she said with near reverence in her voice. ''He's talking to the guest of honor. Ed Dawson almost never attends these things, but he and the Gallaghers go way back. I'm sure the only reason he came is Maggie.''

The man she'd indicated did look very distinguished, but there was something cold about him, a hardness in his eyes that reminded Thea a little of Rick.

Not comfortable with the comparison, she turned her gaze away, and as she did so, it lit on a man in the farthest corner of the room, standing alone. The attire for the evening was casual, but this man's faded jeans were torn at the knees, and he wore his shirt untucked and unbuttoned over a scruffy-looking T-shirt. His brown hair was short and spiked, and in spite of the late hour, he had on sunglasses.

''Who's the man over there?'' Thea said, not wanting to point, although she didn't think he had noticed them sitting on the stairs.

''Who? Oh.'' Meredith lowered her voice. ''That's

Tony. John's youngest brother. He's kind of the black sheep of the family.''

As she spoke, the man reached up and lowered his sunglasses to his nose, staring at Thea over the rims. His eyes were so blue, his gaze so piercing, that she felt a shiver race up her spine.

And she'd thought the Mancusos were dangerous.

Thea turned quickly back to Meredith. ''You seem to know everyone here. Are you a close friend of the family's?''

Meredith grinned. ''You might say that. I used to be married to John.''

JOHN STARTED across the room toward Thea when a hand on his arm halted him. ''John.''

''Miles.''

His cousin dropped his hand. ''Eddie Dawson told me you went to see him yesterday.''

''I figured he would.''

''You're looking under the wrong rock. Eddie had nothing to do with what happened to that reporter.''

John lifted a brow. ''You were there, were you, Miles?''

Annoyance flashed across his features. ''Dammit, John, back off. If you keep pushing Eddie, he'll do the fade, just like he did years ago. And then I'm stuck using some snot-nosed snitch I know nothing about. A man can get his throat slit that way.''

He was right about that. ''Look,'' John said, ''I'm not trying to run off your informant. I'm trying to solve a case here.''

''Which has nothing to do with seven years ago.''

''Yeah,'' John said. ''That's what everybody keeps trying real hard to convince me of.''

"FINALLY," JOHN SAID, plopping down on the stairs one step below Thea. He handed her a beer, draping a casual arm over her knees as he did so. "This okay?"

"It's fine." She took the bottle, cradling it in both hands as she surveyed the crowd. "I just had a very interesting conversation with your ex-wife."

John almost choked on his beer. He glanced up at Thea. "What did she have to say about me?"

"She told me all sorts of interesting tidbits." John groaned and Thea laughed. "I'm teasing. She was just telling me who a lot of these people are. The superintendent of the Chicago Police Department comes to your mother's parties? I'm impressed."

"We go back a long way with his family," John said, his eyes shadowing briefly.

His mother and Nikki came down the stairs just then, and Thea said, "Oh, there you two are."

She took Nikki's hand and tried to pull her down beside her on the stairs, but Maggie said, "Not so fast. We aren't finished yet. We're going to get something to eat, aren't we, Nikki?"

Nikki nodded and followed Maggie down the stairs. Thea sat, almost speechless. Then she said to John, "What is it with you Gallaghers? I've never seen Nikki respond so quickly to people."

"We have our moments," he said dryly.

"Yes," Thea murmured, gazing down at him, "I would say you do."

FIONA WAS THE ONE to bring Nikki back to Thea after a bit. "She's getting really tired. Mom wondered if it would be okay if we put her to bed upstairs until you and John are ready to leave."

Thea chewed her lip, hesitant to allow Nikki to remain out of her sight for much longer. They were standing at the bottom of the stairs, and John said softly, "It'll be fine. We can hang around down here, if it makes you feel better. No one can go up without us seeing them."

Thea nodded, and Fiona led the way up the stairs. She turned on a light, and a blue-and-white room leaped to life. "This is my room, Nikki. I'd be honored to share it with you tonight."

Without hesitation Nikki went over and curled up on the bed with her doll. Fiona covered her with a blue quilt.

Thea had planned to sit with her daughter for a few minutes, but Nikki was already nodding off. She kissed her cheek, and then Fiona took Thea's arm and drew her out of the room. "Don't worry. We'll all keep an eye on her."

"I know you must think I'm an overprotective mother," Thea said.

"And so what if you are?" Fiona demanded. "Isn't a mother supposed to protect her children?"

"I don't know how much John has told you about our situation," Thea said hesitantly.

"Next to nothing," Fiona admitted. "But it doesn't take a brain surgeon to figure out you're in some kind of trouble." She put a hand on Thea's arm. "You can trust John to take care of you, Thea. You and Nikki. He's the best."

"I'm beginning to believe that," Thea said quietly.

"I'm very happy for you both."

Thea glanced at her in shock. "But...it's not...it may not be what you think."

Fiona grinned. "It may not be what *you* think. I see

the way John looks at you. I see the way you look at him, too.''

Thea let out a long breath. ''It's...complicated.''

''I'm sure it is, but I just want you to know that I'm with you. I'll do anything I can to help you and Nikki. She's such a sweetie. I mean, the way she took John's hand earlier when Meredith was acting like such a fool over the baby.'' Fiona rolled her eyes. ''Don't get me wrong—Meredith is okay. John wasn't blameless in that marriage, but he was really hurt when she...left. And then she remarried so fast, and now they have a baby...'' She sighed. ''Oh, well. It doesn't matter anymore. Now he has you. And Nikki.''

Thea didn't know what to say to that, although she didn't feel she could allow Fiona's misconception of her and John's relationship to continue. ''John and I are just—''

''Friends? I don't think so. I've never seen my brother look at a woman the way he looks at you.'' Fiona started for the stairs, then turned back. ''And that includes Meredith,'' she added with a wicked grin.

BY THE TIME THEA CAME down the stairs, John was nowhere in sight. She mingled for a while, but didn't stray far from the stairs. She wanted to be nearby in case Nikki needed her, although her daughter seemed to be making incredible progress. Especially considering last night, when she'd called Thea in the wee hours of the morning. Thea didn't think she would ever forget that moment—the sound of her daughter's voice.

Perhaps it was that memory, or maybe the strong bond between them, that caused Thea to look up precisely when she did. Nikki was standing at the top of the stairs, clutching Piper and gazing down at the crowd in the living room. She wasn't looking at Thea, but at someone—or something—else. The expression on her daughter's face sent a chill through Thea.

She'd seen that look only one other time—when Nikki had stood just inside the bedroom door, gazing down at her father's blood-soaked body.

Nikki had been so traumatized that night that she hadn't spoken since, and now she appeared to be experiencing that same terror again.

Instantly Thea whipped around, scouring the crowd. Her frantic gaze took in all the faces she'd now put names with: Tony and Nick Gallagher. Miles Gallagher and his father, Liam. Superintendent Ed Dawson.

Had one of them frightened Nikki?

Thea sprinted up the stairs and knelt in front of her daughter. The child's face was devoid of emotion, but her eyes were wild looking. She didn't even glance at her mother until Thea caught her arms. "Nikki, what's wrong? What happened?"

The child didn't answer, didn't respond in any manner. Thea tried to think of what could have happened. Nikki had seen someone who had frightened her, sent her fleeing back to that dark hiding place, but who? And why?

Had she recognized someone?

Oh, God, Thea thought. Had Nikki really been on the roof the night Gail Waters fell to her death? Had her daughter seen the killer that night—and tonight?

Fiona had said their father had disappeared, his body never found. What if Gail Waters had been investigating his disappearance, too? What if she'd stumbled onto something that had been hidden for seven years? Hidden...by someone in this very house?

Thea told herself that her imagination was running

away with her, but she couldn't deny that something had terrified her daughter. And if John's family *was* somehow involved, Thea had to get Nikki away from here. They were all cops, and cops stood together. Thea knew that all too well.

She lifted Nikki and carried her back into Fiona's bedroom. She slipped her boots on her tiny feet and laced them. Taking her daughter's hand, she led her down the stairs. They had to find their coats and then somehow make it outside without anyone seeing them.

"Hey, there." John caught her arm, and Thea jumped. "I didn't mean to startle you," he said. "Everything okay?"

She willed down her panic, forced back the urge to tell him what had happened. This was his family. Whose side would he be on if she started making outrageous allegations against them? "Yes, everything's fine. We're getting something to drink."

"Kitchen's that way," he said.

Thea nodded. "Thanks."

But once they were swallowed by the crowd, she picked Nikki up and went down the hallway behind the stairs, where Thea had seen Fiona take their coats.

The bedroom was at the far end of the hall, and the full-size bed was laden with coats. Quickly Thea searched through the pile until she found their coats and her purse. She didn't have much money with her, not enough for her and Nikki to leave the city, but they could at least catch a cab to take them away from this house.

Bundled against the cold, Thea glanced around. They couldn't go out the way they'd come in. John would surely see them. Her gaze flashed to the window. She hurried over and raised the sill. A blast of frigid air slapped at her face, but undaunted, Thea stuck her head outside.

The window was only a few feet from the ground. She could manage the jump, and then Nikki could crawl out and into her arms. It took only a matter of seconds, and then they were both outside, on the cold snowy streets, alone and in danger.

Thea glanced back. The house was brilliantly lit, warm and noisy with laughter. And John was there. John, who would be wondering in a few moments what had happened to them. He was bound to come looking for them.

Thea set Nikki on the sidewalk and took her hand. "Come on, sweatheart. We have to hurry."

But as they ran down the darkened sidewalk, Thea had the strangest feeling that the danger was already following them. That someone, even now, was pursuing them.

Chapter Fourteen

John decided he'd better go rescue Thea and Nikki from the clutches of whatever family member had undoubtedly waylaid them. He hoped to hell it wasn't Meredith again.

Heading for the kitchen, he turned when the front door opened and Roy Cox came in on a draft of icy wind. Not bothering to take off his coat, he spotted John and strode toward him. "We need to talk," he said grimly.

"Back here," John said, recognizing the unusual urgency in his partner's voice. He opened the door of the spare bedroom where his mother always put the coats, but the room was freezing. "Someone left the window open," he muttered, crossing to close it. He turned back to Roy. "So what's up? Why are you so late getting here?"

"The lab called after you left today. That picture you gave them to blow up?" He pulled a manila envelope out of his coat pocket and handed it to John. "Take a look."

They'd blown up various portions of the photograph, including the man's face and his shield. There was something about his dark eyes, something familiar about his features, that made John uneasy.

"I decided to do some checking after the lab had this delivered to the office," Roy said. "I kind of figured you'd been holding out on me."

John dragged a hand through his hair. "Look, I know I owe you an explanation—"

"Save it." Roy traced his mustache with one fingertip. "The guy's name is Rick Mancuso. He's Baltimore PD. Or was. His ex-wife and daughter disappeared about four months ago and haven't been heard from since."

John's heart started to do a slow hammer against his rib cage. "What're their names?"

"The woman's name is Tess Holloway. She took back her maiden name after the divorce. The kid's name is Nicolette."

Tess and Nicolette. Thea and Nikki. Even though he already knew the story, John felt as if he'd been sucker-punched in the gut.

"It's a pretty bizarre tale," Roy said. "It seems this Mancuso guy is—"

"Dead." John glanced at his partner.

Roy scowled. "Dead? Hell, no, he's not dead. He's facing murder charges."

"What?" John said in shock. "Are you sure about this?"

"Yeah. I talked to the guy's lieutenant. Mancuso's been suspended without pay, pending an investigation. See, about four years ago, a man named Donnelli was about to turn state's evidence on the mob, only the guy was smoked before he could testify. An arrest was made, the suspect tried and convicted, but now he's singing from prison that he got a bum rap. Says Mancuso is the one who made the hit.''

"Have you ever met an inmate who wasn't innocent?"

"No, but this guy claims there's a witness. Mancuso was suspected at the time of the hit, but he had at least a dozen witnesses, including cops, who swore he was with them in a bar drinking all night. He claims he never even met Donnelli. But the guy in the joint says that he, Mancuso and Donnelli stopped by Mancuso's house that night before the hit. He says Mancuso's wife saw them all together. She can place Mancuso with Donnelli the night of the murder. Mancuso's ex-wife can finger him if she turns up alive.''

Miles had been right. Gail Waters's death didn't have anything to do with seven years ago. It had nothing to do with John's family, but it had everything to do with Thea and Nikki.

THEY'D HAD TO WALK several blocks before Thea finally spotted a cab, and with every step, she became more and more certain they were being followed. The temptation to simply have the cabdriver keep going was almost irresistible, but Thea barely had enough cash to pay him to take them to the apartment.

Going back there was dangerous, but what else could she do? They had to have money and IDs. Maybe this time they'd even use the passports, leave the country, go somewhere faraway...

And never see John again.

She felt an ache deep inside her at the prospect, but she wouldn't let herself dwell on the pain. She wouldn't let herself worry about what John must think of her, the way she'd run out on him.

She had to concentrate on getting Nikki to safety.

The apartment was dark when Thea let them inside. She didn't turn on any lights. She knew exactly where everything was. She led Nikki to the sofa and said, "Wait right here for me, sweetheart. This won't take long."

Hurriedly she gathered the money from her hiding places—the freezer, behind picture frames, inside a hollow table leg. When she'd collected all the cash, she went into her bedroom to get the passports, stored behind a loose baseboard underneath the bed. Everything was where she'd left it, and she breathed a heavy sigh of relief. She and Nikki were ready to go. They had money, papers—

A sound from the living room stopped her cold. The door had opened, she was sure of it.

But she'd turned the lock behind her and Nikki. No one could get in without a key—

Her mind shot immediately to Morris Dalrimple. He had a passkey.

She heard Nikki whimper, and her blood turned to ice. She lunged for the door, but she was too late. A man stood in the darkened living room, holding Nikki around the waist as the child hung frozen against him.

Thea felt as if the floor had dropped out from under her. Her head spun dangerously, but she forced away the dizziness. Somehow she had to keep her wits about her.

"Hello, darling," Rick said with a sneer. "I'm home."

Thea put a hand to her heart, as if she could somehow slow the pounding. How could this be? How could Rick be standing here in front of her? She'd killed him.

Shot him dead. "Let her go. Please," she begged hoarsely.

"What? Without getting my welcome-home kiss? Maybe you'd like to come over here and take her place."

Thea saw the gun in his hand, then wedged against Nikki's coat. "She's just a baby, Rick. Please. Let her go. This is between you and me."

"You're right about that," he said darkly. "You left me for dead, you bitch." With that, he set Nikki down and she scampered toward Thea.

Thea grabbed her and put her behind her. When Rick started toward them, she screamed, "Run, Nikki. Run!"

She didn't know whether Nikki would obey her or not. The little girl was terrified, just like she was. But almost instantly Thea heard her little feet pounding across the floor, and then the sound of the bedroom door slamming shut.

Rick just laughed. "You can't get away from me that easily. Haven't you learned that by now?"

Without warning he hit Thea across the face with the back of his hand. Her jaw exploded with pain, and she tasted blood as she stumbled backward, crashing against the coffee table before falling to the floor.

Rick was immediately on her, straddling her, pinning her to the floor. "You bitch," he said again, leaning toward her. His eyes gleamed like a wild animal's in the dark.

Thea lay beneath him, not struggling. She was terrified but she had to think. She had to play this smart. Rick wanted her to fight him. He wanted to have a reason to hit her again.

"How—?"

"How did I survive? No thanks to you. You walked away without a qualm that night, blood all over your hands."

"You were going to kill me," she said.

"No, I wasn't," he said. "But I am now."

Thea had no doubt about that. He would kill her, and then he would go after Nikki. The coffee table had collapsed under her weight, and somewhere in the splintered wood lay a glass bowl. If she could reach it...

"How did you get in here?" she asked him.

He grinned. "Your landlord's a little careless with his passkey."

Thea's fingers closed over the smooth surface. Rick was dragging the barrel of his gun slowly down her chest, toying with her, enjoying himself.

"Maybe it doesn't have to end this way," he murmured. "Maybe we could try a little...reconciliation."

When he bent to kiss her, Thea lifted the glass bowl and smashed it with all her strength against his head.

"You...bitch..." he muttered, falling away from her.

Thea scrambled to her feet, then raced to the bedroom door and flung it open. "Nikki! Oh, God, Nikki, where are you?" she called softly, and then Thea noticed the open window. Nikki had gone out on the fire escape, just as they'd done before.

Thea hurried to the window and crawled out. She stood shivering and gazing down at the street, but Nikki was nowhere in sight. Then Thea looked up. Nikki was climbing to the roof. As Thea watched, her daughter's foot slipped on one of the icy rungs, and she clung for a breathless moment until she had her balance again.

Thea didn't dare call out to her. She didn't want to distract Nikki or make her look down. Instead, she started up the slippery steps herself. When she finally got to the roof, Nikki had already disappeared. Thea ran across the deck and tried the door to the stairwell, but it was locked from inside. After Gail Waters's death, Mr. Dalrimple had started keeping it locked.

Where was Nikki? Dear God...

Thea's gaze fell on the rows of drums. She knew instinctively that her daughter was hidden in one of the long channels that ran between the pallets. Thea was small, but she didn't think she could fit. Besides, she didn't want to draw Rick's attention to Nikki. If she could somehow keep him occupied—

Thea turned just as he came over the edge of the roof. He leveled the gun at her. "Nowhere to run to, nowhere to hide!" he sang out.

The wind whipped his words at Thea, and she stared at him shivering. It was snowing, and the scene seemed so surreal that she hadn't a clue what to do.

"Come on out, Nic," he called to his daughter. "You want to save your mother, don't you, baby?"

"No, Nikki, don't!" Thea yelled, but the wind tore the words away. Nikki crawled out of her hiding place and stood facing Rick.

"Leave her alone!" Thea screamed at him.

Rick just grinned as he walked toward them. "I can't leave her alone. She saw me up here the other night. Didn't you, sweetheart?"

Nikki had seen him on the roof? With Gail Waters?

"Why did you kill her?" Thea asked, almost without meaning to.

"That reporter? She'd seen me here in Chicago, too. I mean, I was grateful and all that she'd contacted Baltimore, asking questions about you and Nikki. Not thirty minutes after she called the station I was on my way to Chicago. She led me right to you, but I couldn't have anyone knowing I'd been here. She had to go.''

"You were in her office. You stole the file she had on Nikki and me.''

"I was going to come back here and finish you off then, but you were a little smarter than I gave you credit for. But it was interesting, seeing you at your boyfriend's house tonight. He looks like a real family man, if you can stomach that kind of cop. Nic saw me through the window, didn't you, sweetheart?''

When Nikki didn't respond, he said, "Come over here, baby. Come give your daddy a kiss.''

"You're not my daddy!" Nikki cried, startling both Thea and Rick.

"You little bi—" He made a move toward Nikki, and Thea lurched for her daughter just as the stairwell door flew open. The wind whipped it back with a loud crack. Rick whirled and fired, and out of the corner of her eye Thea saw John stumble and fall to the deck.

Oh, no! her mind screamed, even as her body fell on her daughter, shielding her. She glanced over her shoulder.

Rick stood there, arrogant and defiant, pointing his gun at Thea. She could almost see his finger squeezing the trigger when John fired. The first shot slammed Rick backward, and he stumbled toward the ledge. The second and third shots propelled him over the edge of the roof. He fell without a sound.

Thea wrapped her arms tightly around Nikki, blocking her view. John got up, holding his left arm as he came toward them. He dropped to his knees beside them.

"Are you okay? Is Nikki—"

"We're not hurt," Thea said. Nikki buried her face in Thea's neck, shivering uncontrollably. "It's okay. Shush. It's okay. We're safe now." She looked up at John. "You're hurt. Oh, God…"

"Just nicked," but he winced in pain.

Thea said almost in wonder, "I didn't kill him. I didn't kill Rick."

"No," John said with grim satisfaction. "You didn't."

Nikki turned at the sound of John's voice. When she saw the blood on his arm, her eyes widened in fear and she let out a little cry. John drew her into the crook of his unhurt arm, holding her gently. "I'm okay, kid. How about you?"

Nikki nodded, and then, still silent, she caught a snowflake on her fingertip and touched it to his lips.

Epilogue

Six months later

Spring had come early to the city, perhaps because the winter had been so cruel. Thea, relaxed and unworried, sat on a park bench and gazed at her surroundings. Chicago really was beautiful this time of year.

When the diamond on her finger caught the sunlight and flashed fire, a thrill of wonder shot through her. She and John had been together for six months now. Not *together* together. She and Nikki still had their own place, a new home with a yard and a swing set, not far from John's mother's house.

They'd decided to take things slowly, she and John, and not rush into anything. They'd both made mistakes in their first marriages and were determined not to do the same again.

An early fall wedding had been planned, and truth be told, Thea couldn't wait to be Mrs. John Gallagher. She wasn't sure how she would have made it through that first month after Rick's death without John, when she'd had to go back to Baltimore to testify.

Facing the Mancusos had been one of the hardest things she'd ever done in her life, but John had been by her side constantly. Her and Nikki's. He'd never left them.

And now, in just another few months, they would be together always. Thea's stepmother, Mona, was even thinking of closing down the agency or selling it to one of the investigators and moving to Chicago. Thea hoped she would. Family had become very important to her, and she'd realized just how much she and Nikki had been missing when she'd seen the way John's family had rallied around him in the hospital the night he'd been wounded. The Gallaghers had their difficulties, but it was plain to see how much they cared for one another.

She watched John and Nikki on the playground, and her heart swelled with love. How beautiful spring could be, she thought again, after such a cold bleak winter.

JOHN GAZED DOWN at Nikki. "I don't know if I'm ready for this."

"Come on, Johnny," she said. "Don't be such an ol' fraidy cat."

The kid had definitely been around Fiona too much. John sighed. "Okay. So what's the plan? You first or me?"

Nikki shook her head adamantly. She had come through the tragedy surprisingly well, but she still continued her sessions with Dr. Nevin, and she would for a very long time to come. John had never put much stock in shrinks, but he couldn't deny Nikki's progress.

She squinted up at him. "You stand here," she instructed, taking his hand and placing him at the bottom of the slide. "And don't move."

"You couldn't pry me loose with a crowbar," he said. He watched her climb the steps, his heart in his throat, until she stood at the very top. After climbing three stories to the roof, in freezing wind and snow, this should be a piece of cake, he thought, but he wasn't sure if he was trying to convince Nikki or himself.

She settled herself at the top of the slide, her little legs stretched out before her. "Ready, Johnny?"

"Whenever you are. Let 'er rip."

She sailed toward him, her dark curls flying over her shoulders, her laughter like the peal of a thousand tiny bells. Crossing the bump, she squealed, then glided smoothly toward him, her arms lifted skyward.

He caught her up and swirled her around.

"I did it, Johnny! I did it!"

"That you did. I saw it with my own eyes," he confirmed. Thea came to join them, and he wrapped an arm around her shoulders. "How about that? Did you see what your daughter just did?"

"You're very brave, sweetheart," she said in a husky voice.

Nikki smiled brilliantly and touched her fingertip to John's lips. "Now it's your turn, Johnny."

If you enjoyed what you just read,
then we've got an offer you can't resist!

Take 2 bestselling
love stories FREE!
Plus get a FREE surprise gift!

Back by popular demand are

DEBBIE MACOMBER's

Hard Luck, Alaska, is a
town that needs women!
And the O'Halloran brothers
are just the fellows
to fly them in.

Starting in March 2000 this beloved series returns
in special 2-in-1 collector's editions:

MAIL-ORDER MARRIAGES, featuring
Brides for Brothers and *The Marriage Risk*
On sale March 2000

FAMILY MEN, featuring
Daddy's Little Helper and *Because of the Baby*
On sale July 2000

THE LAST TWO BACHELORS, featuring
Falling for Him and *Ending in Marriage*
On sale August 2000

Collect and enjoy each MIDNIGHT SONS story!

Available at your favorite retail outlet.

HARLEQUIN®
Makes any time special ™

HARLEQUIN®
I N T R I G U E®

43 Light St.

Outside, it looks like a charming old building near the Baltimore waterfront, but inside lurks danger... and romance.

"First lady of suspense" Ruth Glick writing as Rebecca York returns with

#558 NEVER TOO LATE
March 2000

Scott O'Donnell had believed he'd been betrayed by Mariana Reyes, yet he still was unable to resist the attraction that had consumed him six years ago. Their reunion was laced with secrets and danger. With a killer on their trail, Scott had to protect Mariana—and the daughter he never knew he had.

Available at your favorite retail outlet.

HARLEQUIN®
Makes any time special ™

Amnesia...an unknown danger...
a burning desire.

With

HARLEQUIN®

I N T R I G U E®

you're just

A MEMORY AWAY...

from passion, danger...and love!

**Look for all the books in this
exciting miniseries:**

**A NIGHT WITHOUT END (#552)
by Susan Kearney**
On sale January 2000

**FORGOTTEN LULLABY (#556)
by Rita Herron**
On sale February 2000

**HERS TO REMEMBER (#560)
by Karen Lawton Barrett**
On sale March 2000

A MEMORY AWAY...where remembering
the truth becomes a matter of life,
death...and love!

HARLEQUIN®
Makes any time special ™